NO POINTY HATS

Memoirs of a Modern Warlock

By Darrys Aylward

To Pam, without whom this would never have been possible.

Facilis Descensus Averno –

from the Aeneid by Virgil
30-19 BC

The fall into hell is easy

Novitiate

Chapter 1.

If anyone had asked me what my career choices might have been, warlock would not have been one of them. Perhaps airline pilot? Doctor? Mechanic? Any of the above, but warlock definitely not.

It wasn't my idea. Mum saw the job ad and said I should apply. To be honest, I had had enough of stacking shelves in the minimarket and Mum said I needed a better career than that, so I applied.

I didn't think I'd be any good at it, really. I mean, I could do one naff card trick but apart from that, I didn't have what you might call a 'flair for the magical arts,' or indeed, any interest in it.

I think the nearest I'd come to expressing an interest in such things was watching Sooty with his magic wand. It all seemed to be gobbledegook to me and not a subject to be taken seriously.

I don't really know why The Magister took me on. I'm sure there must have been some far more suitable applicants.

Perhaps at least, someone with some acumen for the subject or even a passing interest in the Dark Arts. But me? I was an ordinary boy living an ordinary life, suddenly thrust into the turmoil of magick, hocus-pocus and some very iffy ethical practices.

Notice that I have spelled 'magick' with a 'k'. This is very different from 'magic' without the 'k'. Paul Daniels performed 'magic' – sleight of hand, imagery, abracadabra and all that. I was entering the world of 'magick' – potions, elixirs and spirits.

It would have been nice to have been born in a town with an interesting or intriguing place-name. To be Magister of Dungeonhall or Magister of Grimblewick would have had a much better ring to it rather than the Magister of Maidstone, which doesn't really cut the mustard, as names go. It's a title which sounds more like a pub name than a title for a Master of the Dark Arts.

As you will have gathered, Maidstone was my birth town. Back in the day it was a small market town in the middle of Kent in the South-East of England. I say 'was' intentionally. It's still there – but not as I remember.

It was quite quaint in those days – back in the 60's and 70's. It was an old market town with a wonderful bustling market. Rabbits and ducks hung from the butcher's windows and pheasants and grouse from the fishmonger's windows. There were old buildings and narrow roads and a wonderful smell emanating from the Coffee Importers in Week Street. Like most English towns, it now sprawls and the centre is full of the bland soulless stores which have usurped most towns in modern England – chain stores, nail bars and take-away restaurants. There are exceptions, but Maidstone is not one of them.

I showed no great potential as a child or as an unruly teenager. I had little or no interest in academia – by far preferring to read comics than any great literary works. Like a lot of boys, I would have to consider myself as 'lazy' – at least when it came to reading, writing and arithmetic. My interest was non-existent, much to the despair of my schoolmasters and my mother.

I think it was generally accepted that I would grow up to be one of life's faceless, inconsequential drifters. I was resigned to be as such, with no thought of being anything exceptional in life. I accepted my expected lot.

Filling the shelves of the little minimarket on the Sandling Road seemed to be about my limit. If I had done something similar for one of the larger supermarkets – the likes of David Greigs in Week Street or Safeways in King Street, my prospects might have been more assured. But I was content to work day to day, spending my days filling shelves and my evenings in the good company of the friendly souls in the Flower Pot public house.

Fate is an odd thing – we can't plan anything with certainty. With the best intentions in the world, we cannot change or alter our destinies. What will be will be, and we are powerless to change that. And that is just as it happened to me. Our fates are in the lap of the gods, and my life, whether I liked it or not, was in for a major upheaval.

Mum saw the job ad in the local paper. It didn't say very much, but Mum liked the sound of it, and so I applied, reticently.

'Apprentice required. No experience necessary. Must be versatile and willing to work as and when required.'

That's all it said. I had no ties to speak of – apart from my regular chairs in the Flower Pot or The Dragoon, my time was my own. I had nothing to lose by applying.

I expected the apprenticeship on offer to be pretty uninteresting. I thought maybe knife-grinding on people's doorsteps? Window cleaning? Door to door salesman selling cleaning products? In retrospect, I would have been perfectly content with any of these options. If I had known exactly what I was getting into, I probably would have run a mile.

The interview for the job was arranged in a pub – The Old House at Home in Pudding Lane. I was told to be punctual at twelve midday and to look for a man in a Trilby hat.

Mum fitted me out in a shirt and tie and I duly arrived at the pub at the allotted time.

The man in the Trilby was sat in a quiet corner of the pub, away from the diners and motley drinkers.

He was old, and had a weathered look about him. Smartly dressed with the Trilby hat, which he took off as I approached the table.

He stood and greeted me, shook my hand and sat and looked directly into my eyes. I felt uncomfortable being stared at in this way – but it was an interview after all, so I took it as part of the interview process.

He asked me about myself – how old I was; what my interests were and some general information about my background and family.

He was a pleasant enough man and I began to feel more at ease with him. He wasn't what I would call chatty, though. There was no small talk and as yet no indication of exactly what the nature of the job was for which I had applied.

I had had some training at school in interview technique – most of it was of little use at all. He didn't ask me to sell the ashtray on the table to him and he didn't ask me what my strengths or weaknesses were. Happily so, because I couldn't for the life of me remember what I was supposed to say.

The interview for the job in the minimarket had been a very relaxed affair – could I get up in the mornings, did I live locally and could I add up and take away? I think they were looking for someone reliable rather than with any particular skill set, and the way this interview was going it felt much the same.

Quite out of the blue, my interviewer on this occasion asked "You're wondering what the apprenticeship is all about, aren't you?"

I confessed that I was intrigued – I didn't want to waste his time or my own. I certainly wasn't about to chuck my job in at the minimarket for the sake of nothing.

"I perform magic," he said. I know now of course that he spoke with a 'k' on the end of the word, but at that time I was none the wiser and wouldn't have known what he meant if he had spelled it out to me anyway.

I had visions in my head of him pulling a rabbit out of his Trilby.

"You're imagining I'm about to pull a rabbit out of this hat, aren't you?" He picked up the Trilby and tapped the bottom of it with a broad grin on his face.

How he quite read my exact thoughts was disturbing, yet intriguing.

"Sorry – no rabbits," he said still grinning.

There was something about the man which I found puzzling but enthralling.

"I call it social work," he said, "but not the kind you are thinking of just now."

He was right, I had visions in my head of some kind of counsellor fixing family problems. There were a few children at school who were often absent due to the social workers coming round. I had this image in my head of a slum housing estate, with supermarket trolleys used as garden ornaments and broken children's bikes in the front garden.

"I fix problems," he continued. "It's a unique job role and I won't lie to you - if I was of the inclination to offer you this apprenticeship, there would be a lot of training involved. Not everyone has the acumen for it, nor the inclination to pursue a profession such as this. I need to know if you are the right person for the role before we discuss the work further." I simply nodded in agreement.

"I'll be honest with you," he said, "I have seen other candidates, but none has had the right - how shall I say? The right temperament or train of thought for the role. From what you have told me, you have no preconceived beliefs or opinions, no political or religious leanings, and no distractions. You have sat and listened to me intently without interruption and without a thousand and one questions which I would hesitate to answer. You are a clean canvas – I can work with that."

He sat back into the chair. "This is now your opportunity to ask me whatever you want to ask me. One question – no more, no less. I'll answer you as best I can. Do you want to know how much you'd earn as my apprentice? Do you want to know about working hours, holidays, time off? Do you want to know what training will need to be undertaken? What do you want to know?"

I sat and thought for a moment or two without speaking. Did I really want to pursue this position? What would be the right or the wrong question? Would the offer of the position be reliant on my question? It was a difficult decision on the spur of the moment, but really, I only had one burning question. So, I asked it. Nothing to lose. Nothing ventured...

"How did you know I was thinking about rabbits?"

The man smiled. "I didn't," he said. "Call it an educated guess. "Magic – rabbits. You could've been thinking about sawing a woman in half. I took a guess and got it right. It could've been embarrassing," he said with a chuckle.

"I'm not one to make impetuous decisions," he continued, "and neither are you. You took time to decide on the question you asked me. Take time now and think about my proposal."

He handed me a business card. Apart from the telephone number on the bottom, it contained just three words – Facilis Descensus Averno.

"When you're ready," he said, getting up from his chair, "call me. If you make the decision to take the role, perhaps tell people you'll be doing some research work for some scientist or other? Be vague. There's no need to go into details, not now nor later. Is that OK?"

I nodded in agreement. We walked towards the door. He put on his Trilby, and tipped it to the friendly blonde lady behind the bar.

"Oh, one last thing," he said, "tell your mother she has good taste in shirts and ties."

Chapter 2.

Behind the High Pavement on the Sandling Road lies a labyrinth of narrow roads and terraced houses. Not built with cars in mind, the roads now are all but impassable, but in the 60s and 70s most residents did not have cars so there was room enough for those living there. A short walk into town did not require any form of transport.

Tiny shops in front rooms were dotted about the area – only the residents knew where most of these were. Placards stating 'Walls Ice Cream' or 'Golden Virginia' gave the game away as to their whereabouts.

Behind a nondescript terraced house within this tangle of streets and doorsteps, I found myself in what from the outside, looked like a somewhat outsized garden shed. For the size of the backyards packed with washing lines behind the houses – the shed was far too big. We reached the shed via a narrow-arched alleyway between two terraced houses. I learned later that the shed was rented from the elderly lady who lived in the house to the right of the passage.

The inside of the shed was not what I had expected to see. I anticipated a dark and musty room with herbs hanging from the ceiling and jars of animal body parts and obscene ephemera on dusty and decrepit shelves. I couldn't have imagined in my wildest dreams a white-tiled and immaculate laboratory!

There were stainless-steel workbenches, high-stools also of stainless-steel, a white linoleum floor and cabinets of multiple small, white drawers, each labelled with symbols, not one of which I recognised. A large fridge was positioned in one corner and a machine, which looked to me very much like a Flatley Clothes Dryer, was neatly snuggled into the opposite corner. All other available wall spaces were occupied by white Formica shelving and a myriad of different jars containing nothing remotely recognisable and labelled with similarly weird and wonderful symbols.

There was very little 'on show'. Everything was ordered, out of sight and tidy, all exposed surfaces being intensively and extensively cleaned.

"Not matching your expectations, is it?" the Magister asked.

I acknowledged that this was indeed the case.

"Cleanliness," the Magister said, "is not next to Godliness. "Cleanliness is a religion all of its own."

He explained the importance of spotlessness. There are dangers in cross-contamination - a trace of something here and a drop of something there can result in chaos. And we were in the business of putting order into chaos.

I didn't really know what he meant at the time, but I came to realise he was right.

He showed me around the Sanctum Sanctorum – a term I had yet to fully understand. He called it the 'Sanctum' for short, which was a bit easier for me to comprehend in my novice state.

Each of the little white drawers contained herbs or spices in different stages of decay. Every individual drawer was divided into four narrow sections. Every section bore one of four symbols, which the Magister explained to me: the first was an empty circle which symbolised a new moon; the second bore a crescent directed to the left which represented a waxing moon; the third a black circle – a full moon and the fourth a crescent directed to the right – a waning moon. These represented the time when the herb or spice had been collected. The symbols on the outer drawers represented a herb, a spice, a mixture of herbs or spices, or both.

The inside of the fridge housed the collection jars I was expecting to see on my initial entry. All the jars were labelled with symbols and filled with unrecognisable contents.

From what I had seen so far, I could perceive that I was about to embark on a steep learning curve.

"I have taken the liberty," the Magister said, "to enrol you in a Herbalist Correspondence Course. You can either study here or at home – the choice is yours. However, if you choose to study at home, I would expect you to achieve some privacy in your work."

I agreed it might be better to study in the Sanctum. Home could be noisy and boisterous and not really ideal for learning. My failed exams were testament to this – oh, and my general laziness.

He gave me a book – 'The Modern Herbalist' which was the go-to book for the Correspondence Course.

"It's yours," he said. "Feel free to make notes in it."

He then passed me a hard-backed note book, on which he had written 'G1'. I asked what that meant.

"Grimoire One," he informed me.

The book was lined and margined. The Magister suggested that I should use one page for each herb studied, and to add the symbol for the herb (which he would tell me), adding the herb's usage and misuse and other notes which might prove to be useful.

"This envelope contains a description of the course," he said, handing me a large brown envelope, "and your first lesson. I don't need to see the work you do in relation to the course – your remote teacher will correct you or advise you when and where necessary. But each week I will ask you what you have learnt – it's not a test – it's to see if further understanding is required."

His proposal seemed reasonable, so I assented.

"The course is expected to take one to two years," he explained. "It won't permit you to practise as a qualified herbalist, but it will give you a good grounding in herbs and their potential use in general medicine. Other applications for the use of the herbs, I will tell you in good time."

He rummaged through a drawer in the work bench and pulled out another large envelope.

"And this," he said, tapping the edge of the envelope on the table, "is where the hard work begins." He passed me the envelope. "Don't be dismayed," he said, "we all have to start somewhere. Open the envelope. Don't be alarmed."

I took the book from the envelope. My heart sank. 'A Beginner's Guide to Latin' was not what I was expecting.

I had taken French at school but was thrown off the course after a French exchange student taught me some words which I used to try to impress the teacher. I didn't know the meaning of the words I had used – I only repeated parrot-fashion what the boy had told me. But using them got me suspended from school, a smack from my mother and my removal from all language teaching in the school. And that was the end of my foreign language education. I didn't think that 'Jean-Paul est dans la rue' would be of much help to me now.

"I can see you're not impressed," the Magister said. "Don't be fazed by it. It's really not so bad when you get your head around it. I'm afraid that an understanding of Latin is crucial to our work. There is no getting around it. But don't worry – if you can determine the general principles of the language, it will become easier as you progress through the workbook. I'm here to help – I struggled, too, at the beginning – it's like second nature now."

I was not convinced and was starting to think I had made a mistake agreeing to take on this apprenticeship.

The Magister tried to allay my fears.

"I was a young man, just like you," he said. "I was largely uneducated, with preconceived judgements about my abilities – or disabilities to be more precise. I was told I would be proved wrong and I'm now saying the same to you. Until your potential is realised, you have no idea what you might or might not be able to achieve. I have total faith in you – I would not have taken you on if I didn't believe in you. You will learn in time the power of belief. I need you now to believe in yourself – to believe in your own potential. Belief is the key."

He made me feel better about it, but I wasn't strictly convinced. 'Fine words butter no parsnips' my mother used to say. I was in dire need of some butter for my parsnips.

"Now," he said, "put your books away for the time being. We'll take a look at them together this afternoon." - A little reprieve from the daunting prospect ahead of me. "Each morning, I will ask you to get some bits and pieces together which I will need for the day ahead. This will allow you to become familiar with what we have here. The application for their uses will become clearer in time. For the moment, I want you to concentrate on familiarising yourself with the various symbols and ingredients. I'll give you quick example. If I was to tell you that the symbol for rosemary is a circle centrally positioned above two parallel lines, please could you find for me a sprig of rosemary which was picked on the waning moon?"

I looked over the lines of drawers and found the symbol as he had described. I opened the drawer. I remembered what he had said about the phases of the moon, but found the fourth compartment for the waning moon empty.

"Excellent!" the Magister said. "I'll make a note that that is missing and will need to be found. See? Not as daunting as you first thought, is it?"

I agreed that that seemed simple enough. "What are the two drawers either side of this one?" I asked, pointing at the two drawers either side of the drawer containing rosemary. Both had the same parallel lines, but the circles above the lines were to the left and the right.

"I am delighted, young man," he said, "already a thirst for knowledge. I'm impressed. All in good time, though. One thing at a time." He gave my shoulder a little squeeze. "Now," he said, "I need you to get me something else."

I was ready and keen for the next instruction.

"Nip down to the bakers, will you? I don't know about you but my tummy's rumbling. Get us a couple of sausage rolls each, will you? I could eat a scabby horse."

I could feel myself starting to feel strangely at home and pleased to be in this unfamiliar place.

"Don't let me catch you smile like that too often," he said, "I'll have to dock your wages." We both laughed.

I was unexpectedly at ease.

Chapter 3.

Days turned into weeks which became months. I was getting a good grasp of the various ingredients we used and the symbolism associated with them.

Any vertical line through a symbol conveyed an element of risk associated with it. It didn't mean that the element was necessarily poisonous, but meant 'caution'. A vertical line at an angle from right to left indicated the thing should not be ingested and from left to right meant 'could cause an allergic reaction'. Only very few symbols had two vertical lines struck through it, and this implied extreme caution, such as the symbols for henbane or hemlock.

Getting my head around these symbols was easier than learning yet another weight system. In 1979 we were just getting used to the metric system of weights, but many shops still used the old Imperial system of pounds and ounces. I now had to learn a new system – actually an old system, but one which was new to me. This was the so-called Apothecary System of weights and measures. Instead of pounds and ounces we used a system whereby twenty grains equalled one scruple; three scruples equalled one drachm and there were eight drachms to the ounce. Unlike the Imperial system whereby sixteen ounces equals a pound, in the Apothecary System, there are only twelve ounces to the pound.

Most of the ingredients the Magister required were measured in grains or scruples, being small in volume. So, if he required a certain herb for the day's work, he would write the symbol for the herb, followed by the moon phase symbol followed by the weight symbol, be it the symbol for grains or scruples. Rarely did he use the symbol for a drachm. We only used small amounts of each herb.

I would put each ingredient in a small glass bowl and line them up in the order the Magister had requested. I soon got used to the symbols and weights, and if I got one of the ingredients or weights wrong, he would tut-tut around the Sanctum, putting it in front of me saying, "Try again." He never reprimanded me even on those occasions when I got things very wrong. He would fly into a temper if *he* made a mistake, but was exceptionally patient with me.

The Magister carried on with his work. I had no knowledge what he needed these ingredients for or what he was making or why or for whom. Such things were not as yet disclosed to me.

After I had arranged his required items for the day, I would apply myself to my studies. I slowly learned what he might be doing by looking out the corner of my eye.

There were infusions – herbs or other ephemera infused in hot water. These, I had decided, were like herbal teas, but I could have been mistaken. There were the ointments which looked like they were oil-based, and creams which were more water-based. Potions were for skin application and elixirs were for ingestion, in a liquid or tablet form. Emollients had the same appearance as the potions but contained different ingredients. I wasn't 100% sure which was which, but the more I watched the more familiar I became with the differences.

Most unusual of all to my eye were the aromatics. It wasn't altogether clear how or what these might be used for. He had a special piece of equipment for this. It consisted of a large glass jar which he heated by means of a little camping stove. He half-filled the jar with cold water and dry or semi-dry ingredients, corked the jar and left to simmer over a small flame — sometimes for hours on end. I never saw the final outcome neither did I see how the aromatics were bottled.

I have a confession to make — I had a growing loathing for Latin. I knew it was a crucial part of my training, but knowing that didn't help me to adjust to it or have any kind of affection for it. The Magister tried to encourage me, but I couldn't help but feel he was trying to flog a dead horse. "Ad astra per aspera" [To the stars through difficulty] he'd say, adding to my annoyance that I couldn't understand the meaning behind what he was saying.

Sometimes, he would leave me to my studies and venture out. I knew when he was about to meet up with a querent as he would wear his Trilby hat. The hat was like his calling card — it allowed others to know who he was without actually announcing his presence.

One such day he went out and came back in a foul mood. He didn't reveal the cause, but told me to go home early and to be in at seven in the morning sharp. I did as he bid me without question – whatever the reason, a half day is a half day and I spent a very pleasant afternoon enjoying the summer sunshine in Brenchley Gardens.

My mother had started asking questions. I didn't like lying to her so I bent the truth as far as I dare. Friends who asked me what I was doing I could lie to with no qualms. But then my two worlds of home and work collided, and I found myself caught between a rock and a very hard place.

My brother turned eighteen. He is two years my junior and being a special birthday, my mother decided we needed to celebrate.

A table for three was booked at the Wig & Gown – my mother's favourite restaurant. The Wig & Gown was a trendy pub and restaurant across the road from Maidstone Prison and County Hall, and just a stone's throw from the town centre. By today's standards, the Wig & Gown was old-fashioned, but for its day it was seen as the in-place to be, and similar to the Running Horse just a mile and a half away, was a popular place for people of all generations.

My brother had the misfortune of being born on Valentine's Day – unfortunate, because on Valentine's Day, restaurants were full of courting couples, and married people who sat in silence eating their prawn cocktails, steaks and Black Forest Gateaux. As eateries still do now, restaurants inflated their prices with a 'Special Valentine's Menu' when there was nothing special about it except for the price. Everybody knew it was a rip-off, but men desperate to please (or appease) their girlfriends or wives were happy to pay the overblown prices.

Mum chose the nearest Saturday to his birthday (which was Saturday 17th February) to have the celebratory meal – belated, but did it really matter? Not to most reasonable folks, no, but to my brother it was something of a disappointment – no, not a disappointment, he took it as a slight - he wasn't worth the extra cost of having the meal on his actual birthday. Needless to say, this was the last ever attempt to take him out for a birthday meal.

That week, there was a definite air of tension between my brother and mother. I was glad to not be involved in the awkwardness of the occasion and just went with the flow, happy to be going out for a celebratory meal, for which I would not have to pay.

I'd often heard it said that 'you could cut an atmosphere with a knife', but hadn't experienced that feeling until now.

My brother, rather than be happy and grateful for this little freebie treat, acted like a petulant child and sat grumpy and cold, picking the prawns off the lettuce one by one.

My mother, rightly so, was exasperated. She turned the conversation to me and my life to try to make light of the situation, ignoring my peevish brother.

"You work near here, don't you?" she asked, smiling through gritted teeth.

"Not far," I said. "Up the road a bit." I pointed in the general direction of the Sanctum.

"Which road?" she asked. "It's like a maze round there."

"Near to the allotments," I said, trying to sound specific without giving any actual details.

"My friend, Mrs Tennett, lives round there. I can't think I've seen anything like a research facility around there. Apart from the brickworks, it's all houses. What does the building look like? I might know it."

"There isn't no research facility around there," my brother interjected as he flipped a prawn onto the tablecloth.

"It's hidden," I explained. "You can't see it from the road."

"What do you do in there?" my brother asked, abruptly. "And don't tell me 'research'. 'Research' my arse! Trust me, it's something dodgy."

"Mind your own business and eat your prawns! Your brother's speaking!" my mother snapped back at him.

"I can hear him speaking in foreign in his room," my brother added. "Research my arse!"

"Mind your tongue!" my mother interjected brusquely. "Carry on, dear," she said, "don't mind him. You were saying?"

"I wasn't," I said, looking like a rabbit caught in the headlights. "You know I can't say anything – it's a government thing."

My mother looked at me with a sidewards look, like she did if I ever lied to her. I might be studying the mysteries and wonders of the universe, but how mothers know when you are lying is an enigma never to be solved.

24

"Government?" my brother questioned, sneering. "You're just full of it. Mark my words, it's something well iffy."

"It's nothing iffy – I just can't talk about it. Most of it is just filing at the moment."

A tap on my shoulder interrupted me. A friend from school was standing behind me with his latest girlfriend in tow.

He introduced us to the girl who I remembered vaguely from primary school. I thought I was off-the-hook from answering questions.

"We saw you, didn't we?" My friend asked for corroboration from the girl, "On Snodland Marshes. We were in one of the hides, birdwatching."

My brother choked on a bit of lettuce. "Hahaha – birdwatching!" he said, laughing. "Is that what they call it now?" My friend and the girl both blushed.

"I was doing some research work," I said.

My brother regained his breath and continued to chuckle.

"Oh!" my friend said, raising an eyebrow. "It looked to us like you were picking some wild flowers, didn't it?" The way he had to continually have his story corroborated by the girl was annoying. The girl said a very quiet 'yes' and smiled at her boyfriend.

My brother let out a loud laugh. At least he had broken out of his bad mood. "Wild flowers?" he said, laughing and snorting. "Wild flowers! Oh my God, this is too funny. Wild flowers!" He put down his spoon and fork and got out the words "Oh, for God's sake, I'm going to have to go to the toilet."

We could hear him laughing until the door closed behind him.

"Well," my friend said, "we'd better leave you to it. I couldn't get time off on Wednesday, so this is our Valentine's meal."

Mum and I both said we hope they'd have a nice evening. My brother was still not back from the toilets. My mother's face said it all.

"You said you were doing filing! What the hell were you doing picking flowers on the Snodland Marshes? There's something you're not telling me. Are you telling me lies? Is there something going on I don't know about? Are you doing something dodgy like your brother said?" She sat waiting for an answer, arms folded, staring at me intently.

"Sorry, Mum," I said. "It's not something I can tell you about. I wish I could. Just believe me when I tell you there's nothing dodgy, nothing illegal, nothing remotely iffy going on."

"If you ever, and I mean *ever* lie to me again, I'll have your guts for garters!"

My brother returned and apart from the occasional giggle from his direction, we sat and finished our meal in silence. Happy Birthday.

Chapter 4.

I told the Magister about the problems I had with my family.

"Mmm...," he said, "I experienced much the same thing when I started out. They'll stop asking eventually. Do you know that building on the Sittingbourne Road – the Department for Agriculture Fisheries and Food?"

I said I had seen it.

"If they ask again, tell them you're working in a subdivision of that. I suppose you realise that gradually you'll become somewhat estranged from your family, don't you? There is a price we have to pay for doing the work we do – it's part of the sacrifice for our way of life. Family, social life – it can all take a bit of a thrashing in time."

My family never asked me again, but at least I had an answer at the ready if they did.

It was now 1981 and the face of Maidstone was changing. I got the distinct feeling I was being left in the past. The Vinters Park Estate was no longer considered to be a 'new build' and the atrocity of the Stoneborough Shopping Centre was killing off the smaller shops in Week Street and Earl Street. Bistros were replacing cafes, and pubs became restaurants almost overnight. Butchers stopped hanging up rabbits and game birds outside their shops so that people weren't offended. As long as the meat didn't look like the animals it came from, people were happy to eat it. Brown eggs replaced white eggs in some bizarre notion that they were healthier, and featureless road systems were trading places with the old historic streets which were so familiar to us.

I had completed the Herbalist Course within a year and a half – not with flying colours but receiving a pass certificate which earned me an extra £5 a week. In 1981, £50 a week was a good wage, even more so for an apprentice. The Magister suggested it was time to start looking for my own place to live in and to progressively sever ties with my former life.

I still struggled with my Latin studies, but sluggishly persevered.

"I don't want an answer from you straight away," the Magister said, "but I want you to think about this: a man comes to you in a distraught state. He has not had intimate relations with his wife for many months. He has found out that his wife is having an affair with his brother. The man wants to wreak vengeance on both his wife and his brother. What might be your response? Don't tell me now. Think about it."

This was my baptism into some of the work of the Magister and the perplexing world of ethics associated with it.

I gave his question a lot of thought. There was a lot to consider, and truthfully I wasn't prepared anywhere near adequately to answer it. We could quite easily put a hex on the wife and brother, but this was not the answer the Magister had in mind.

I understood from what the Magister had previously told me that life is a balance. Not of good or evil but a balance of give and take. It isn't possible to have something without paying for it – not in monetary terms but in a matter of sacrifice. To coin a phrase, you cannot have your cake and eat it, too. If this man in question wanted to punish his wife and brother, there would be a price to pay for doing so.

The Magister gave me this example: a woman is deeply in love with her neighbour and wishes to attract him to her with the idea of making him her husband. What might she be willing to sacrifice to procure this? Yes, she could pay us to create a potion for her, but that would not be the cost involved. The universe is a balance – she wouldn't be able to have her man without sacrificing something else.

The Magister continued to explain. "Sacrifice is a complicated subject and not easily understood, or more often than not, it is misunderstood. When we think of sacrifice, we bring to mind someone in days gone by, buying a goat to sacrifice to which ever deity required it in exchange for their help. Whatever the deity needs it for, is not a question, although probably it should have been asked - many a poor, defenceless goat could have had their lives saved. No matter, that is not the point. If the person who is making the sacrifice can afford to do so in a monetary sense, it is no sacrifice. There is no exchange of values. There is no balance.

He continued, telling me the Bible story of the 'Widow's Mite'. I had no interest in Church matters or Biblical rhetoric, but the story made sense. The widow couldn't afford to put any money in the collection plate - to do so would result in not being able to feed herself or her children. Others could afford to give generously and piled their money in – usually in clear view of others to show off their supposed altruism. The widow put in the tiniest of coins, which she couldn't afford to do, but did so for the greater good. She made a sacrifice while the others who gave much larger sums of money sacrificed nothing. Someone going on a diet cannot sacrifice chocolate to lose weight, as there is no balance – the sacrifice benefits the sacrificer. There can be no benefit to the sacrificer in the sacrifice. To do so can cause an imbalance.

I was beginning to understand, but I was still a little confused and I strongly suspect it showed on my face.

Returning to the woman who wants to attract her neighbour, the Magister asked "What could she sacrifice to realise this? Her friends? Her freedom – could she find herself in a loveless and troubled marriage? Perhaps the neighbour is a habitual gambler, infertile or a womaniser? What is she really willing to sacrifice to get her man? Querents must always be told that a sacrifice of some sort will be required. This is mandatory – they must be made aware before we help them. Someone who says they'd give their right arm to be wealthy, may, without realising it, be speaking literally."

The Magister becomes an adviser. "Certainly, the woman could be given a potion to allure the man and a hex could be put on him to enable this, but she must be aware that sometimes there can be a heavy price to pay to achieve what she wanted."

The question the Magister had asked me about the man, his brother and his wife was not a practical question – it was a question of ethics.

A couple of weeks later, the Magister asked if I had had time to consider his question.

"The man has already lost his wife to his brother. To take her back would result in a loveless marriage, full of hate and despising. If the wife preferred his brother, there would be no point in trying to win her back anyway. The relationship with his brother is unlikely to mend – the damage to his family has already been done. I can understand the man's desire to punish them, but the punishment might have already been issued. Perhaps this was a matter of lust, and between the adulterers this can age and diminish with time. Without some secure ad deep-seated emotions within their relationship, the relationship is likely to fail, having already destroyed the joy they might have otherwise possessed had they not succumbed to their passion.

"What would the man be willing to sacrifice to wreak vengeance on the couple? Perhaps a lonely future awaits him, estranged from his children and the rest of his family. Perhaps destitution – he could lose the roof above his head. The question is not how he can wreak vengeance, but what he is willing to pay for it."

"I like your train of thought," the Magister admitted. "Ethical questions are the hardest to answer, but the querent has come to us to help him. What might we be able to do for him?"

I had an answer, but wasn't sure if the Magister would agree with it. "Don't worry," he said, "there is no right or wrong answer. I just want to know your way of thinking. Tell me what you might do in this instance."

"I've given it a lot of thought," I told him. "The best vengeance I could see for the man would be to create an unhappiness – a fissure - in his wife's and brother's dalliance. I think the man wants them to feel as low and dejected as he feels. He has had his happiness and security already taken away, so to wreak vengeance would not exact a sacrifice. This would restore balance."

"So?" The Magister was keen to know my conclusion.

"It should be feasible to induce a cosmetic appearance of venereal disease, shouldn't it?"

"Yes," the Magister agreed. "So how might we do that – create the appearance of venereal disease without actually inducing the condition?"

I said I really didn't know. "Well," he said, "what might a herbalist use to if not cure, ameliorate the condition?"

I knew from my studies that usual treatment would be a concoction of aloe vera and propolis. Propolis is a material made by bees for building their hives.

"And what is the symbol for aloe vera?" I knew that the symbol consisted of three horizontal lines with a circle and a star above the lines. "And propolis?" I wasn't sure. "Take a look in the fridge," the Magister said. "There is a small jar marked with a single horizontal line and two crosses to the left, above the line. Crosses indicate that the propolis is creature-derived. And what if the symbols were turned upside down?"

"Well," I surmised, "the inverted symbol for the aloe vera is common nettle." I didn't know what the inverted symbol of the propolis might be, only that it would be creature-derived.

"No – you wouldn't know that. It's formic acid – ant venom." I could now understand how the salve might work. The penny was beginning to drop.

"So," I concluded, "both the wife and the brother could be led to believe that they had contracted venereal disease from the other, when in actuality, no disease is present. All it would take would be to put a smear of the salve on one or the other's undergarments. This would doubtless lead to arguments and disruption between the two miscreants, resulting in a fissure in their relationship, destroying the joy they thought they once had. But their relationship would have been purely physical, and anything to put an end to their desires would annihilate their affiliation. The only winner in this respect would be the husband who had been wronged."

"I like it," the Magister said. "Now, let us make the potion. Get me a clean bowl, will you please?" This was the first time I had been shown how to make a potion without just surreptitiously watching from the corner of my eye.

While we made the potion, the Magister said "There is a symposium for novitiates about to take place in Cambridge. I think it would be of great benefit to you. How do you feel about going to it?"

I had nothing to lose, so I agreed to go. "It's a two-day symposium," he explained. "Don't worry about it – you have done well and will probably be far more knowledgeable than some of the other participants. Sorry it's such short notice – it's planned for next Tuesday. Will that be a problem?"

I had no other commitments other than work and studies and I was looking forward to meeting other novitiates. Up till then, I wrongly had the impression that I was the only person undertaking this training. I was looking forward to it.

Chapter 5.

I'm not sure quite what I was expecting from the symposium, but a small room with just six chairs in it wasn't what I had anticipated at all. Everything I had so far witnessed in this profession had shattered any preconceived illusions I might have had.

There were all five of us novices and the Magister. The Magister of Cambridge was younger than my Magister and was a cheerful soul and far more animated. He liked to crack jokes and was exceptionally friendly and warm in his greeting.

We novitiates were roughly all the same age, give or take a year or two. There was one lad from the North East, a girl from Wales, a Scottish lad, myself and another from Brighton – who was to destined to become a friend for life. I nicknamed him 'Pinky' after the character created by Graham Greene in his book Brighton Rock. Pinky said it wasn't fair as he didn't know of anyone from Maidstone.

We were all put up in a little guest house near to the city centre, so we got to know each other reasonably well during the two-day course. We were a friendly bunch. The girl from Wales came over as being a bit aloof and didn't appreciate the banter and repartee. She was more thoughtful, obviously very intelligent, and I think we all felt a bit too flippant around her - but each to their own. She fit in as best she could.

We shared stories of our Magisters and the awful mistakes we had made during our internships and discussed some as yet unexplained phenomena. We had all expected a wand to be used somehow or other, but this was not the case. Or at least, none of us had seen one. We asked the Magister of Cambridge why that was.

He laughed. "It sounds like you still have in your heads some old-fashioned notion of what the Dark Arts are," he said. "Perhaps some of you still have a memory of Mickey Mouse splitting brooms in half?" He continued, "In the olden days, the wand was a phallic symbol – usually made of a long stick of wood – which the witches hid in twigs, to conceal their forbidden beliefs. This is where the idea of witches flying on broomsticks comes from, that and the use of some powerful hallucinogens. Nowadays, rather than using a wand, we use a finger to point at things. It's much easier and you don't have to carry it around the place. A dried stick is of no use whatsoever. A pointy hat isn't of much use either. Unless your head tends to get cold and you have particularly high ceilings, of course."

We enjoyed his sense of humour and were grateful to him for answering some of our questions we hadn't dared to ask our Magisters. "Don't be slow in asking your Magisters questions," he advised. "The Magisters are there to be your guides. Allow them to guide you."

"We will be covering two subjects on this symposium," he explained. "Should you have any questions, interrupt me at any time, so long as the question is relative to the subject being discussed. Any other questions - feel free to ask, but perhaps leave them for coffee or lunch breaks. You will not need to take notes." The girl from Wales put her notebook and pen back into her handbag.

"I want you to consider this news article I have here." He waved a newspaper cutting in his hand. "This is a true story which was reported in the Manchester Journal in September two years ago." He cleared his throat and read from the paper. "'On Tuesday last, police report a road traffic accident in Baylam Road, Salford, involving a young mother and her four-year-old son. The boy was playing with a neighbour's son in the front garden of their house, being watched by his mother from the front room window. As they were playing, a milk float collided with a transit van, the van veering off the road into the garden of the house, pinning the woman's child underneath the nearside front wheel of the van. The neighbour's child escaped unscathed. The woman ran out from the house and saw her child in what could have been a life-threatening condition. Without assistance, the woman lifted the van off her son and turned the van on its axis so that the boy was completely free. Police who reported the incident could not come to any conclusion how the woman was able to achieve this feat of superstrength. A spokesman is quoted as saying 'It took four officers to remove the van to the side of the road, without lifting it. How the lady managed to lift it clean off the child and move the van towards the pavement is something of a mystery. Following a check-up at hospital, the boy was discharged with only superficial injuries. The van driver has been charged with reckless driving. The driver of the milk float was reported to be shaken but otherwise unharmed.'"

I didn't look at the others, but I could only imagine that they had the same expression of perplexity on their faces as I did.

"Can any of you suggest how this might've happened?" the Magister asked.

One of us suggested that the woman had a momentary boost of strength, another that perhaps it was the angle of the van which enabled her to lift it.

"The answer," he said, "is simpler than that. The answer is 'belief'. For one solitary moment, without thinking about it, without wondering if it could be done, without doubting herself, without any notion of failure, the woman believed she was able to lift the van and was able to lift it away from her child. Belief is by far the most powerful tool we have at our disposal, and belief is the cornerstone of everything we do."

He continued. "Let us be clear, 'faith' and 'belief' are not one and the same. 'Faith' includes a notion of trust and an element of doubt, whereas 'belief' is a certainty with no element of hesitation or uncertainty. Take as an example - you go mountaineering. You can put your faith in the rope that could save your life, but not your belief. To 'believe' in the rope would be foolish – it could fray, break or not hold onto its tether. You could not 'believe' the rope would save you. You put your faith in the rope, not your belief."

The lad from the North-East raised his hand. "You do not need to raise your hand. Yes – what would you like to ask?"

"If there is a difference in 'faith' and 'belief', what is 'blind faith'?"

"Good question, thank you. Going back to our analogy of the rope, to have blind faith in the rope, you foolishly put your faith in the rope without checking it first. You don't check the rope, the condition of the rope or the rope's tether. You haven't experienced a problem with the rope before, so you put your blind faith in it. Remind me not to go mountaineering with you! Oh, and by the way, most adherents to organised religion, any religion, have blind faith in their chosen creed, not belief."

The Magister certainly had our attention. He spoke in a very down to Earth way with good and clear examples of what he was talking about. Did I have faith in him? Did I believe him? Or did I have blind faith in him? Mmm... food for thought. Answers on a postcard please...

"So, how can we use 'belief' in our work? Let me put it like this – I'm sure you will all have heard about the placebo effect? A patient puts his trust in a doctor to help him and is given a tablet to cure him or relieve symptoms. The patient doesn't know whether he has been given the medicine or a placebo, or if there are placebos at all. The results tend to be the same. Alternatively, a tablet or placebo can be used to create a symptom – the result is also the same. This is because the patient 'believes' the tablet will have the reaction expected.

"When we use placebos in our work, we call this 'dissonance'."

The Magister gave this example: "A man is down on his luck. He is becoming estranged from his wife; he hates his job; his children rarely speak to him and he feels that the world in general is against him. First of all, we'll discuss the possible causes for the man's feeling of abandonment and hopelessness."

We all came up with different ideas as to what the man's problems could be caused by. These ranged from someone putting a hex on him to a medical condition.

"These are all viable possibilities," the Magister said, "but look at the facts again. Marriages are hard work. Has he really made the commitment to his wife – or indeed has she to him? He hates his job – that can be easily changed to something he prefers to do. His children rarely speak to him, – does he give them the time to speak to him or is he so wrapped up in his own negative feelings that these are passed down to his children resulting in In his increasing isolation? What becomes clear by taking a step backwards and looking at things from the outside, is that there is a distinct lack of effort on the part of the man. He's not working on the relationships with his wife and children, workwise he is stuck in a rut and he has become worn down by his own lack of verve. The feelings the man has that the world is against him is misjudged. In reality – it is him against the world, not vice versa. What could we do for this man? Your answers after the break, please. Time for lunch, I think!"

A sandwich lunch awaited us and Pinky and I sat chatting. Other little groups were forming amongst the students, with the exception of the girl from Wales, who seemed to prefer to sit alone. The Magister interrupted us. "I couldn't help but overhear your conversation," he said. Then he spoke to the whole group.

"Can I ask how you are all doing with your Latin studies?" A groan went up from all of us. "I thought that might be the case." He must have heard everything we were saying.

"Latin isn't the easiest of things, is it? I've just heard these two" (he pointed to Pinky and me) "saying they weren't sure of the reason for having to study Latin."

That isn't exactly what we were saying – we were having a good old moan about it.

"The thing is," he continued, "we use Latin as grammatically it is more precise than English. There is less room for ambiguity – the meanings of the words and their placements within a sentence are more rigid – reducing the possibility of error. Latin is also widely used as a universal language in our work – you could take a grimoire from just about anywhere in the world, and the symbolism and hexes would be much the same. Do persevere with it. I confess that I was the laziest ever student when it came to my Latin studies and this put me back in my apprenticeship by two or three years."

Then he changed tack. "I don't know if you are aware," he said, "but your apprenticeships are nearing the end of the first stage in your training. When your Magister is quite certain you are ready, you will be put forward to take your Peritus Examin. The Peritus Examin consists of three papers – the first will test your knowledge of herbs and other ephemera, symbols, their uses, inverted uses and so on. The second paper concerns matters of ethics and the third is a Latin paper. It is only quite recently, and by 'recently' I mean 'within the last two hundred years or so' that the Latin exam is a written paper. Before this, it was an oral exam – so count your lucky stars for such small mercies. Should you pass the exam, you will be given the title 'Adept' and will be given a new professional name with the letters ADA after it – Adept of the Dark Arts. Although the title 'Adept' gives you some privileges, this will not allow you to work unsupervised and will only allow some access to spiritualia. But we'll talk more about that tomorrow. Meanwhile, keep up with your Latin studies – you are going to need them."

We spoke in hushed voices after that.

In the afternoon, the Magister went into great detail about the art of dissonance. We were asked for our opinions about the scenario he had told us before – the man who felt he was becoming isolated from his family.

The girl from Wales raised a good point. "You're quite right," the Magister said. "We have an ethical duty to suggest to the man that he seeks medical advice first. It could be that he is suffering from clinical depression and could need professional help. I think this is a rule of thumb – if anyone approaches you with any kind of medical condition – physical or mental, it is important to refer them to professional help. We are not healers and we are not qualified to speak as such. We merely put order into chaos."

The Scottish lad suggested that the man could 'tether himself' to his family. I had heard about 'tethering' or 'binding' but wasn't altogether familiar with the technique. 'Tethering' involves a form of meditation whereby someone can emotionally tie themselves to other people – not by any physical means but by metaphysical stimuli. "The problem with tethering in this instance," the Magister explained, "is whether that would make the man more content, or could it make his feelings of isolation and despair worsen if he comes to feel it might have been better to simply walk away? 'Tethering' is notoriously difficult to undo if you think you might have made a mistake and wish to become untethered. Perhaps he could be tethered and then at a later date, meet someone new with whom he feels he could be happy. Maybe not the best answer in this situation."

The rest of us had nothing to add to the suggestions already put forward.

"What this man needs," he explained, "is to realise that he holds the key to solve his own problems. But how can we help him to see that?" No-one ventured an answer. "Let's set the man a challenge. Let's set him something so difficult to do he can begin to believe in himself."

He drew from a black velvet pouch a small, ornate glass phial. "Have any of you seen one of these before?" he asked. None of us had. "These are special phials, which we use in circumstances such as we are discussing," he explained. "In itself, it is not anything special – it looks special, but in reality it's just a cheap glass phial, but when handed to a querent it looks to be special and to their mind will contain something extraordinary and unique. Truth is, all it will contain is some water with a foul-tasting but harmless essence. Remember – the more foul-smelling or tasting something is, the more powerful the querent thinks it is. Belief is crucial. Keeping the phial in a black velvet pouch adds to the mystery of the contents.

"So, our stage is set with this simple concoction which contains nothing of any benefit whatsoever. At this point the querent must be told to tell no-one what it is you're going to tell him. This is a contract between you and him. To tell others will diminish the power of the phial. It gets more special by the minute, doesn't it?. Hahaha." We all laughed at the clever deceit.

"So we could just have the man drink the contents of the phial, but except for a bad taste in his mouth, it will achieve nothing. What we're going to do, is we are going to create a challenge for the man. It will go something along the lines of this: 'Tell no man what it is I tell you.' Remember to speak slowly and clearly and in something of a lower tone than your usual speech. Do not shorten words but speak in full English. For example, do not use 'you'll' but instead 'you will'. Generally, we don't speak like this, so it will create a subtle message of sincerity and importance. Hch hm, sorry – we'll start again. Hch hm... 'Tell no man what it is I tell you. In this pouch is a phial of potent elixir. Do not remove the phial from the pouch until you are ready to do so. This and the information I will give you is for you only.' If you want to add a few choice Latin words when you pass him the pouch, feel free to do so. 'Ego do tibi hoc vitrum' - it only means 'I give you this glass' – but see how impressive this sounds to someone who doesn't have a clue what you're talking about? Using a lower tone and speaking slowly gives the impression to the querent that something extraordinary is about to happen. Sorry – I keep on getting side-tracked. Where were we? Yes, thank you, so we

43

pass him the pouch and have told him not to tell anyone. 'You will go from this place and on the next moon, you will seek out a willow tree which is growing beside the water.' Most towns and cities have rivers and most have willow trees growing beside the water somewhere along the banks. People can have a strange foreboding about full moons without knowing why - they associate a full moon with werewolves and all kinds of nonsense. Nine bob to a pound they'll go and find a willow tree long before the full moon – but no matter. Sorry – I just need a glass of water. You tell me what happens next – what could we tell the man to do? Be back in a moment."

The Magister left the room momentarily. You could see from our faces we were thoroughly enjoying this lesson.

"Come on then," the Magister beckoned, "hit me with it. What you got?"

The Scottish lad spoke first. "We could have him take off his shoes and socks and stand in the water, recite some words and drink the elixir, then throw the phial in the water?"

"Yes, very good, but not really a challenge, is it?"

The other lad from the South coast was next up. "He could skim a stone to the other bank of the river?"

"Mmm.. not bad, but it's still not much of a challenge, either, is it?"

I suggested "He could take an empty bucket with him and he could fill the backet with water from the river with his hands."

"Yes, I like that. Perhaps he could stand knee deep in the water at the same time. I think we're getting there."

The Welsh girl piped up, "He could do that while chanting," she said. "The challenge in my mind, would be him trying not to explain to passers-by what on earth he was doing. He'd look like a mad man."

"I like it!" the Magister said. "After all this, the man will feel he has achieved something and will believe he has turned his life around. He will be ready to make changes for the better."

We discussed the matter of dissonance, and then before we finished for the day the Magister said, "When you come in tomorrow, bring nothing in with you. No teas, no coffees, no half-eaten breakfast sandwiches, no handbags, notebooks or pens. We need a clear room. Have a good evening!"

///

Following our evening meal, the others from the group sat discussing the day's work. Pinky had different ideas. "Come with me," he said, and beckoned me outside.

There were some cast irons stairs outside the communal room in the guest house – a fire escape - where we sat and Pinky lit up a cigarette, drawing on it deeply. "I've got something to show you," he said, with a mischievous glisten in his eye.

We could see the group sat inside. The girl from Wales was reading a book; the guy from the North-East was watching the small TV, the other lad and the Scottish lad were chatting and laughing, drinking tea.

"Watch him!" my friend said, pointing to the Scottish lad, while he stubbed out his cigarette on the side of his shoe.

"What am I looking at?" I asked. "He's just sitting there drinking a cup of tea."

"No," he said, "he isn't. Watch him. He's holding the cup with two hands. The fingers of his right hand are curled around the handle and the forefinger and thumb of the left hand are supporting it. The other fingers of his left hand are curled under the left forefinger in a relaxed position. Notice when he takes a sip – he purses his lips and rather than taking the cup to his lips he leans forward towards the cup without moving his shoulders, just his neck, stretching it towards the cup."

I watched as the lad did exactly that. "What of it?" I asked.

"Just keep on watching and study his movements," he said. "Look at his feet - the right foot is curled under the chair, resting on his big toe. The foot is swinging on the big toe. The other foot is flat on the floor. Look at the distance between his feet. Watch – he's taking a sip. Did you see the way he looks over the rim of the cup staring straight ahead when he sips? And then he leans his neck back again into a relaxed state. His left elbow is digging into his ribs, which in turn supports his arm and hand which supports the cup. He's going in for another sip. Now, look at what I'm doing."

He arranged his feet in the same formation and his legs were at the same angle as the Scottish lad's. He held a make-believe cup, holding his hands in exactly the same way and he mimicked the way the lad was sipping his tea. "He shifts his centre of balance as he takes the sip – shifting from the right hip to the left hip. There he goes again looking over the rim of his cup at nothing. Now watch!"

He positioned himself into exactly the same posture as the Scottish lad. As the lad raised his cup and his neck arched slowly forward towards the rim of the cup, my friend, in a sudden movement, dropped his imaginary cup. In perfect synchronicity, the Scottish lad dropped his, his jaw agape in wonder as to how he could have dropped the cup so unexpectedly and for no reason.

My induction into the darker side of magick was complete.

Chapter 6.

The mood the next morning was very different from the day before.

"Silence!" the Magister called out as we entered the room. The room was dark apart from a single white candle which stood in the centre of a bare wooden table. Our chairs were ordered around the table. There was nothing else in the room.

"Silence!" the Magister repeated. "Silence!" he barked out at us with asperity. We took our seats in silence and the Magister closed the door, then sat in the chair at the head of the table. None of us dare speak. This was a very different Magister from the one we had seen previously. There were no jokes and no good-natured repartee.

"Today," he said, "you will learn one of the most serious tenets of our profession. Beware!" I wished he would stop making us jump – we were all becoming nervous. He spoke in a hushed voice, and then boom! All our hearts missed a beat.

He could read us with great clarity. "Do I make you nervous?" he asked. "Good! If I can make you nervous, half of my job here is done." At this point, I don't think one of us wanted to be in the room with this man. 'On edge' didn't quite cover it.

"What is a spirit?" he asked us. "And no, it isn't the essence of a dead person. We are not in the business of communing with the dead – we leave that to the mediums and the charlatans. Spirits are not dead. Spirits are living beings but in a different form from ours. Theirs is not a tangible world and yet they live among us. They feel; they have purpose; they can communicate with us and with each other. Most important lesson of all you have to learn today, is that spirits *lie*." His emphasis fell on the word 'lie', booming it out making us jump again. He leaned forward and looked at us intently, one by one.

He took a newspaper cutting out of his trouser pocket. "Not the most reliable of journals, but I am going to read to you from a cutting taken from Psychic News." He cleared his throat. I think we all hoped he'd finished doing with the sudden shouting. He could see we were all on edge.

On the night of July 14th last, a disturbance was reported at Cedar Grove, Thornton Cleveleys. Police and an ambulance were called to the address, following the sound of screams emanating from the semi-detached house.

After entering the property, police found two girls aged sixteen and seventeen in a distressed state. A third girl, nineteen, was found in the middle of the road outside the house. All three girls were in a profound state of shock.

The three girls had been playing with a Ouija Board. One of the three girls told the police the following: "It was just supposed to be a bit of fun. We'd done it before and nothing much happened so we thought we'd try it again. We were sat with our fingers on the glass and it started to move. My sister called out 'Is there anybody there?' and the glass just went to the sign 'NO' and wouldn't do anything else. So, all three of us called out if there was anybody there and still the glass ran around again and pointed to the word 'NO' for the second time. It didn't make any sense, because if there was nobody there, how could the glass move? Again, we called out and then the glass began to move. It went all over the place, not spelling out anything decipherable. It was like the glass was out of control then it stopped dead, and went no further. Try as we might, nothing could get the glass to move. Out of the blue, when we were near to giving up altogether, the glass began to traverse the board. At this point, only I was touching the glass. The glass spelled out 'FRIEND'. Excitedly, we put our fingers back on the glass and the word 'GAME' was spelled out. It seemed to be quite fun, so we continued. Next, the glass spelled out 'WINDOW BIRD'. We opened the window and looked out. There on the window sill was a robin. We closed the curtain again. Next, the glass moved and spelled out 'DOOR DOG'. We went to the door, opened it and my dog was sat there, patiently waiting for us. The spirit was playing a game with us. Next, the glass spelled out 'FONE'. The phone rang – there was no-one on the other end, but it had rung all the same. Lastly, the glass spelled out 'DOOR DOG' again. We opened the door and to our horror my dog lay dead on the carpet. We were horrified. We all screamed. At this point we all panicked. The glass started to move without us touching it. We watched as the glass spelled out 'YOU NEXT' and then we totally lost control. My sister was screaming uncontrollably and our friend ran out of the house, yelling as she ran, narrowly missing a passing car.

All three girls were treated for shock and the Ouija Board was destroyed.

"Spirits lie!" The Magister repeated. If you take nothing other than this from today's lesson – remember this – spirits lie!"

We all felt a bit unsettled. Our discomfort was quite clear to see – we were in trepidation as to what was going to happen next.

"We need to ask ourselves," the Magister continued, "why do spirits lie? What could a spirit possibly gain? Of course, there is a flip side to this and one which can be even more noteworthy – sometimes they tell the truth and that can be more alarming than if they lie."

I don't know about the others but I was getting confused. "That news article you just read out to us," I asked, "the spirit did lie as the spirit was not friendly, but it described itself as a friend. But then, it told the truth – the bird at the window, the telephone, the dog at the door. How could anyone know what might or might not be the truth or a lie?"

"Good question," the Magister answered, "you don't. And that is the point. Believe nothing, trust nothing, doubt everything."

He continued, "Four of the most dangerous words anyone could possibly ask are 'Is there anybody there?' There most certainly will be. The better question would be 'Who is there?'"

We all had a myriad of questions. The Magister did his best to answer them. 'Why do spirits exist?' 'What do spirits want?' 'Are spirits good or evil?' The questions came faster than the Magister could respond.

"Spirits exist. From whence they come or why they come is open to conjecture. Some people claim to have the answers, but in truth they only *think* they have the answers. Nothing in this world is clear cut, the spirit world even less so. Nothing is pure good and nothing is pure evil. Everything is a shade in between, and spirits are no exception."

The Magister went on to explain. "When we evoke a spirit for whatever purpose, we do not really evoke it. The spirit is already with us. What we do is to ask the spirit to present itself to us. Some spirits (as we will see shortly) are happy to oblige us and present themselves readily. Others are reticent to show themselves, and then others can dominate a gathering. What we have to ask, is why has this spirit presented itself? Is it there to assist us or does it have its own agenda?"

He went on. "In a similar vein, what do you want from the spirit? Be clear about your purpose. Just asking a spirit to present itself with no reason will probably result in failure – or worse. Be mindful – spirits are not here to amuse us – they are not some kind of circus act entertaining us for our benefit. They are living beings and deserve respect. They must not be abused." He paused. "If any of you are not comfortable with these proceedings, or simply do not wish to continue, please leave now."th

At this point, both the Welsh girl and the Scottish lad left. Both said this was not for them and they went out of the room and did not return.

"Are we happy to continue?" the Magister asked. Those of us remaining nodded our consent.

"Watch the candle," he instructed. "The candle is not here to create ambience. The candle can tell us a lot about what is going on at the time. Sit still and watch the flame." He spoke to me directly. "From where you are sitting and without leaning forward, blow gently towards the flame." The flame bent away from me and a couple of drips of wax trickled down the length of it. "It is quite clear from which direction the flame was manipulated – from East to West. Well, East to West – ish – not exact, but that's not the purpose of this exercise. Now watch…" The flame flickered – not from any specific area. "In this instance, there is a dispelling of the flame - this indicates an energy in the room – not from any direction in particular. Now watch…" The flame burnt brighter and then dulled. "So, the flame burns brighter the nearer the source of energy and more dimly when the energy is further away."

The Magister smiled. "Holy Spirit, declare yourself!" he said as the candle flickered. "Guys," he said, "meet Jonas. Jonas is a trusted spirit, aren't you Jonas?" The spirit made a knocking sound somewhere in the room, but it was not possible to determine exactly where the sound came from. "Jonas is here as a training guide. He is quite used to helping us in this way." Something brushed against the back of my neck and I flinched.

"Don't mind him," the Magister said, noticing me jump. "Just a little game he likes to play." I could see from the other two novices they too felt the same thing.

"Right, Jonas," the Magister said, "time for our lessons. With the help of Jonas, we will try to find out what other spirits might be here. Jonas is our trusted guide and will tell us if any other spirits are present and if we should be wary of them, whether they are friendly or helpful, et cetera. Brace yourselves!" The Magister grinned from ear to ear.

This was one day I definitely would never forget. Jonas introduced us to two more spirits – one more friendly than the other.

To the spirit who was likely to cause mischief, the Magister simply said "Spirit be gone!" and that seemed to be the end of it.

All three of us had so many questions and the Magister tried to answer them. I asked him about how to protect ourselves from mischievous spirits and suggested a circle of salt to protect us. He laughed. "You watch far too many movies," he said. "What good would salt do, exactly?" I felt a fool for asking it. "It is other spirits in whom we trust that provide us with the protection we need. They can alert us to danger and as you have seen, most unwanted spirits can quite easily be dispelled. Some not so much, but this is something you will come to learn in good time."

He continued. "You will be allotted your own spirit guide as your novitiate training proceeds. Don't be in too much of a hurry to achieve this. Your Magisters will guide you through the process – it is not something I can do here. Jonas is one of three spirit guides I have access to."

Pinky said "Please can I ask, what do you use them for?"

"Mmm.." he pondered. "We don't *use* the spirits as such – the word 'use' in this context is erroneous and the spirits could take offence. We can ask for their advice or their insight. Say for example, you are dealing with a complicated case – perhaps a querent wants to know why he is being overlooked for promotion at work. We could possibly deduce the answer – perhaps the querent simply isn't good enough for the position they are after, or perhaps their boss has a favourite, or even nepotism comes in to play? There are all sorts of reasons for this to be happening. A spirit can help us to see the situation with greater clarity – there could be all sorts of mischief afoot, or not as the case may be. The spirit can guide us as to how best to deal with the situation. Does that make sense?"

It sort of did and sort of didn't make sense. "You will understand in good time," he said.

The Magister explained that questions for the spirits are not asked in words but in images. He showed us how to ask a question in this format and how to interpret the answers the spirits gave. This was a similar technique as that used in dream interpretation – a phrase can be transposed into an image. For example, the image of somebody standing at the edge of a swimming pool without going in could be interpreted at being reticent to 'take the plunge'.

The training continued well past our five o'clock finish time.

As the day's training drew to a close, we said our goodbyes and Pinky and I swapped phone numbers. "Stay in touch!" he said and I made my way to the train station.

Chapter 7.

I returned to Maidstone with a renewed vigour. Meeting other novices, and in particular making friends with Pinky, had done me the power of good. I went back to my studies with a regenerated drive.

I took a lease on some rooms in the basement of a house in Peel Street. Although not happy about me moving out, Mum helped me to decorate and furnish the little flat. It was quite light for a basement apartment and I had access to the garden, yet seldom used it.

My new fervour didn't go unnoticed. The Magister taught me the art of potion making and hexing. He began to include me in some of the work he was doing, explaining what he was doing and why he was doing it. It wasn't until the Spring Equinox that the Magister suggested I go with him on a consultation.

"You will need to wear something distinguishable and identifiable," he suggested. "What do young people like to wear these days?"

Well, we weren't much into wearing hats of any ilk. Flares and platform shoes had long since been consigned to the dustbin, denim was in and corduroy and cheesecloth were out. I suggested wearing a stud in an ear, to which he agreed. "Have something that stands out," he said, "you need to be seen and identified. Maybe a pearl or a ruby or something like that?"

I assented. There was a beauty parlour up by Maidstone West train station I had seen which did such things.

I had a burning question to ask him while we were readying ourselves to go out and meet a client. "I hope you don't mind me asking," I said sheepishly, "but what is the significance of the feather in the band of your hat?"

The Magister took off his Trilby and looked at it. "There are many mysteries in this universe and to some I have answers," he said, "but this is not one of them. I bought it like that." He laughed heartily and I cringed to have asked such a pathetic question. He tapped me in a friendly gesture on the shoulder. "Thank you," he said. "It's not often I laugh these days!"

We had arranged to meet the querents at The Bull pub on Penenden Heath. We could have taken the bus up the Boxley Road, but it was a nice day and the Magister suggested we take the scenic route on foot instead.

We walked along the Sandling Road and took a cut up through the corner of the Army Barracks and thence onto Sandling Lane, up past the Cuckoo Woods to Penenden Heath, and then on to The Bull, which was on the opposite corner to where the town gallows once stood. Whenever I saw the place where miscreants had met their demise for stealing a sheep, I couldn't but wonder - if I had been born two or three hundred years previously, I might have met my own untimely death there.

The Bull was a grand old pub with a public and a saloon bar. I had spent many an evening in the public bar as a teenager, but was not so familiar with the cosiness of the saloon. Like so many other local pubs, The Bull is now a restaurant and is not designed for the friendly, rowdy nights I enjoyed in my youth.

We had time to chat during our little walk and he answered a lot of the burning questions I had building up inside, other than about the feather in his hat. I was curious as to how querents were able to find him – how did they know such a service existed? It wasn't as if we could advertise our services in the Yellow Pages.

"Word of mouth, primarily," he explained, "but some referrals come to us directly via Head Office." The Head Office he was referring to was the Magisterial Association of Diviners, which was the head-quarters of the Chief Magister – the Magister Princeps of the UK. Head Office was known affectionately as the MAD House. I didn't know where the place was located, but had it in my head that it was in the Midlands somewhere – or possibly the North? I wasn't sure but it didn't really matter.

"Why do we meet querents in such public places?" I asked. For something which was supposed to be of a veiled nature, such openness seemed to be a contradiction.

"It makes people feel comfortable," he explained. "Querents can be very nervous – they have no idea what to expect when they meet us – it puts them at ease meeting in a public place."

He went on to explain that some people have the idea that we would turn up in tall, pointy hats and great cloaks covered in weird and wonderful symbols. "Sometimes, they almost seem to be disappointed," he said, "but we change that with an air of aloofness. I'll show you – you'll see. It's all about keeping an air of mystery and detachment. The Royals do exactly the same thing – they thrive on the air of mystery surrounding them – we do much the same but not from such ornate carriages," he said, laughing.

The Magister made it clear that we do not answer any personal questions or any questions about our profession. "It's on a 'need-to-know' basis," he said. "There is nothing they need to know, so there are no questions we need to answer. It's like being a politician – let the querent think they are being told something when in reality we tell them nothing at all. We let the querent think they have some say in what we are going to do for them, when in reality we hold all the ace cards and allow them to do nothing; but we don't let the querent think that. You'll get the gist. When we get in there, sit and listen, nod when you think it appropriate, but say nothing. Let the querent see that you are deep in thought. Give the impression that you have a deep insight into their predicament and the solution we have to it. Never let on that you are shocked or confused or that you disagree with them. Never ever laugh, no matter how bizarre or outrageous their request appears to be. Give them your best 'poker face'!" he said, and laughed. It was nice seeing him so cheerful. I think the pleasant walk up to the Heath did us both good.

The couple sitting in front of us were, as anticipated, nervous. I sat silent and the Magister spoke to them. He introduced me to them as his 'associate'. The married couple tried to make small talk, but the Magister was adamant and resolute not to do so. They asked if we were local, what our names were, had we been doing this long and all manner of inappropriate questions, none of which were answered.

"I'm sorry to get to the point," the Magister said, "but we are on something of a tight schedule today. What seems to be the problem?"

They apologised for taking up our time and told us their story. They had lived at their current address for the past ten years or so and had always got on very well with their neighbours on both sides. New neighbours had moved in across the street from them and at first, all was well and they had become friendly with them. However, in a short period of time, friendliness had turned into over-familiarity. The new neighbours had started calling round at all hours of the day and sometimes quite late at night – always on the pretext of needing something, telling them something, or sometimes just 'for a chat and a cup of tea'. Their visitations were daily and sometimes several times a day. They had nothing against the neighbours and didn't want to appear to be rude, but the constant visits were becoming annoying and had caused the couple to start to bicker with each other – each blaming the other for encouraging these visits. The neighbours never knocked or rang the bell, but would just walk in calling out 'It's only me!' as they walked through the door.

Push came to shove when the male querent's mother had died that morning and the neighbours came in asking to borrow some garden tools. The female neighbour made them all a cup of tea without being asked to do so, then sat for three hours talking about nothing in particular. The couple had grieving to do and phone calls to make of a personal nature.

When they asked the neighbours to leave so that they could do what they wanted and needed to do, the couple make another cup of tea instead, saying 'a cup of tea was what they needed' and proceeded to discuss their upcoming holiday to Majorca.

The querents had had enough and told the couple to get out. This had the effect of the woman neighbour saying 'Ah, you're upset – of course you are. We'll come back tomorrow when you're feeling better.' They left half an hour later and it was at this point the querents decided that something needed to be done and that these unwarranted social calls needed to come to a stop.

The Magister sat listening intently to the querents' case and when they stopped talking sat quietly, as though deep in thought for a minute or two, which can seem like an age when you're waiting.

"We can help you," he informed them. The weight lifting from their shoulders was almost visible. Their faces relaxed and both breathed deeply.

The male querent asked what it was we could do. The Magister said "Have faith in our ability. What we can or cannot do is not suitable for discussion. If you trust us to help you without causing any further problems or repercussions, then allow us to do so. I will need some photographs to help us," he said. He explained that we would need some photos of the front door inside and out; the back door inside and out; the front garden gate from both sides and good quality photographs of the couple they wish to dissuade from visiting.

"You won't do anything to them, will you – the neighbours, I mean?" the man asked. I don't know quite what he thought we might do – kill them? Poison them? I've no idea.

The Magister looked the man up and down with an emotionless face. "None shall be harmed," he said and left it at that.

The couple agreed to provide the photographs and payment within a week. It was explained to them that once both were received, the job would be done and they would be able to get on with their lives.

We left the pub and walked back the Boxley Road way.

The Magister had taken to asking my opinion on the odd occasion and this day was no different. I told him that I didn't think the neighbours were solely to blame for what was going on and that the querents probably encouraged the behaviour. The querents were probably not getting on very well before this happened, and used the neighbours' frequent visits to detract from their own problems.

The Magister agreed and asked what cause of action I would take if I was in a similar situation. My own option would be to give the neighbours the 'cold shoulder'. Without being nasty to them, I would make them feel decidedly unwelcome until the visits fizzled out. I said to the Magister that I didn't see why the querents didn't do something similar.

"You're quite right of course – that would be the logical solution. Very good. But we are not necessarily dealing with people who are used to using logic, are we? We have this 'thing' in British culture of not wanting to offend or be rude towards others. By and large, that is the way we do things and to give someone 'the cold shoulder' as you so aptly put it, goes against the grain with us."

I had a burning question that I had been waiting to ask for months. "I noticed a while back," I asked, rather sheepishly, "you don't lock the...Sanctum." I nearly called it the 'shed' but corrected myself just in the nick of time. "I don't know how you do it, but are you planning to use the same method to keep the neighbours away?"

"Well deduced, Dr Watson," he said and laughed. "Yes - it's similar. With the Sanctum, I simply keep everyone out, but allow you access. It's quite simply done, and we'll do something along the same lines with this case. Pardon – I need to correct myself – you'll do this one. Don't worry – I'll take you through the method step by step."

"What would happen if someone tried to access the Sanctum without your authority?"

"Apart from me cutting off their fingers with a carving knife," he said, alarmingly, "absolutely nothing. Nothing would happen. It is a matter of my mind versus their mind. I've already won the battle even before they knew there was a war." He could see I was still looking a bit alarmed about the carving knife thing.

"Chop, chop, chop," he said, moving his hand in a chopping motion and laughing. It was good to see him in such high spirits. "And call the Sanctum 'the shed' again, and it will be chop, chop, chop for you!" He had a raucous, gravelly laugh which was a joy to hear.

"Mmm," he continued as we went on with our walk, "just thinking out loud here – we could do with somewhere to do this training," he said. "We'll need somewhere nice and quiet to concentrate with a bit of comfort as the process could take a while – the Sanctum doesn't quite cut the mustard, does it? What do you think about using your place for this? How would you feel about that?"

I said it would be fine but wasn't sure on a level of one to ten just how comfortable he might find it. "Have you got chairs?" he asked.

I confirmed I had chairs. "Well then, there you go," he said, cheerfully. "We'll wait for the photos and then we'll see to it."

I agreed that that would be perfectly acceptable. I'd have to borrow Mum's Hoover beforehand, though. Hopefully it wouldn't be too soon or a regular occurrence.

"You provide the tea and I'll provide the doughnuts," he said, laughing as we walked.

Chapter 8.

A couple of weeks later, three envelopes were waiting for me on my workstation in the Sanctum. The first contained the photographs of the querents' doors and neighbours together with their cash payment. We used a PO Box for our post, postmen in general not delivering to sheds in gardens. The second contained a hand-written letter from Pinky and the third contained my application forms to sit the Peritus Examin.

The Magister hadn't told me he had put me forward to take the exam, but discussing it with him later that day, he convinced me I was ready to sit it. "You'll trip up with the Latin, I know you will, but the rest will be a breeze for you," he told me. He estimated I would receive a total of 95%, the pass rate being 90%. I asked about what would happen if I passed the exam. "That will very much depend on Head Office," he said. "They will give you your new name and will suggest a new path for you, depending on your strengths or weaknesses shown in the examination. They might suggest a path you hadn't even contemplated, or they might just leave you here, working alongside me. They're pretty good at getting such things right."

I had assumed that my path would have continued with my Magister. I knew I still had much to learn and I also knew that the Magister was keen to show me much more than he had done already. "Don't worry about it," the Magister advised, "you will have options – it's not as if you will be given an order to or go somewhere or do something you don't want to do." He went on to explain that if I passed the exam successfully I would be paid directly from Head Office, and in effect would work under their direction and not the Magister's.

The letter from Pinky was a boon. He had invited me to spend some time with him after I had sat the Peritus Examin, which he was due to sit at the same time as me. This seemed like a great idea and the Magister said I had earned the break and that it would do me some good to see how the Brighton Chapter operated.

"I'm not over-familiar with the Brighton Chapter," he said, "and I would urge caution. There could be 'factions'."

I asked what the 'factions' could be. "Well," he said, "there can be a variance in method and some Chapters rely heavily on tenets not necessarily condoned by Head Office." He went on to explain the controversial aspects of the Ordo Templi Orientis, the Golden Dawn and the Rosicrucians, amongst others. "Keep an open mind," he advised, "and take nothing as fact or at face value. Learn but do not be influenced – Facilis Descensus Averno." I knew the meaning of the words – it is easy to fall into Hell – but I was still learning the profound meaning of the quotation.

The forms for the examination were pretty standard and were completed and sent off the next day.

"We've nothing else pressing," the Magister said. "Will it be convenient if we run through the 'Gateway Procedure' this afternoon?" He was referring to the technique of barring admittance to a premises.

I said it was fine and we arranged to meet up at my rooms at one that afternoon. He let me go off early that morning 'to prepare'. I guess he thought the place could probably do with a quick spruce up before he arrived.

The Magister arrived promptly at one and commented on how pleasant my rooms were. They were basic but clean and since about twelve o'clock that day, tidy.

Cups of tea made (accompanied by some non-existant doughnuts), our training started more or less straightaway.

"I'm going to train you how to think," he said. "Not only to think, but to concentrate at a level you've probably never achieved before. I'd be interested to know," he asked, "have you ever made an Airfix model?"

I told him I'd made a couple. I didn't tell him my efforts were somewhat haphazard, I always had parts left over and the wings on my Spitfire didn't stay level, but that wasn't what he'd asked me.

"When you do something like that, you need to exercise a great power of concentration – handling tiny parts and manipulating the glue or a paintbrush. You can become totally absorbed in such an endeavour. I never did quite master it myself – all fingers and thumbs, but I found the concentration required to perform the task enlightening. My old Magister had me make an Airfix model before teaching me this procedure – but I don't think that was entirely necessary."

I could see what he was getting at – I remember sitting up till midnight trying to get a wheel to stay attached, unaware of the time I'd spent on it. In the end, the whole fire engine went in the bin.

He asked if there was anyone I didn't want to visit my rooms. The only person I could think of was my brother. He'd come over once before and proceeded to look and comment on everything I owned, which made me feel awkward and uneasy.

"OK," the Magister said, "I can understand that. Right – I want you to close your eyes and picture the outside of your front door." I didn't have a back door so that made it easier. "Now, picture it in every detail. Do you need to look at it again, properly this time?" I said I didn't as I'd only just recently painted it and knew all the marks and dents there were to know. "Picture yourself inside the door, looking out from the open door. Now back outside again looking at the closed door. Get the two images clearly in your mind. Every flaw, every blemish - picture them inside your head. Alternate between these two images. Now picture your brother standing looking at the closed front door from the outside. I assume you know how your brother looks without having to see an image of him? Good. Try to add into the image of him any little quirks there are about him. A necklace maybe, or an earring, or is there something he always like to wear like a hat or a scarf?"

I pictured him with the silver crucifix he liked to wear on a silver chain, which my mother had given him for his eighteenth birthday. There was a grey t-shirt he wore more often than not, so I pictured him wearing that as well.

"Now, go between the image you have of your brother, standing looking at your closed front door, as though you are the door looking at him. You're not inside anymore, you are becoming the door in front of him. I can see from the way you're frowning you are concentrating intently in producing these images. Deepen your concentration. Relax the muscles in your forehead. You are a door. You are no longer yourself. Note your breathing rhythm. Breathe in deeper and exhale slowly – become the door. Nod when you tell me the image is fixed entirely inside your head. Continue to breathe deeply and relax the muscles in your face. A door doesn't have emotions. Clear all emotion from the image you have created. Ignore any feelings either positive or negative you may have about your brother. Your brother is an image and you are a door. Breathe slowly and deeply. When you feel ready, I want you to enter into the images you have, a fire - a bright, blazing fire in between the door and your brother. Breathe deeply. Feel the lack of emotion and the emptiness of everything around you. If you're ready, insert the blazing fire in between you – the door - and the image of your brother. The fire doesn't singe you or your brother but it blazes brightly, yellow flames turning white with the heat. Watch as the flames burn. Watch the image of your brother back away from the heat and brightness of the flames. Breathe deeply. Continue to watch the image in front of you. Watch as the image of your brother melts away, further and further away from the flames – so far away now that if you were to reach out towards him, he is too far to touch. His image is now in the distance, moving further away all the time until you can see his image no more. Your brother is gone. Continue to breathe deeply and when you feel ready, you can open your eyes."

I felt fatigued. The light hit my eyes when I opened them, dazzling me. It was as if I had not been present in the room. I had become the door. I sensed that I felt strangely different. I would say I felt 'other-worldly', but that sounds cheesy and not accurate. I was perfectly at ease and not stressed in any way, but I was drained of energy.

"Exhausting, isn't it?" the Magister said nodding. "It can really take it out of you. Please don't look at the clock – how long did that procedure take you?" I guessed it was a few minutes but was alarmed to hear that it had taken nearly an hour and a half. "Time disappears when you truly concentrate, doesn't it? Time no longer exists – it evaporates in front of you."

He then showed me the photographs the querents had provided and we discussed how best to create the same image of the doors and the neighbours.

"We'll do it tomorrow," the Magister said. "You need rest. I've done this for years, but I don't think even I could do two in a day – it really takes it out of you. Take the rest of the day to recuperate and look at it fresh-faced tomorrow. Perhaps get those exam forms filled in, if you get chance?"

I agreed to do that.

My brother never did come round to my flat again.

Chapter 9

The first of the three exam papers was a simple matter of recognising symbols, explaining their uses and their inverted uses. It also included the creation and use of simple tinctures and potions which posed no great problem.

The second paper concerned matters of ethics, and of the three papers I found this the trickiest. There were three scenarios offered, one of which we had to choose to answer. Ethical arguments were expected and possible outcomes and solutions outlined. The first ethical question was a matter of infidelity; the third was a querent wanting to put a curse of impotency on a work colleague, and the second, which seemed the hardest question, I chose to answer.

It was about a housing estate which was experiencing anti-social behaviour from some of the residents. Gardens had been trashed, residents harassed, litter thrown everywhere and there had been incidents of common assault. The main perpetrator was a fifteen-year-old boy, so legally a child, and therein lay the ethical question. An adult would be fair game for some forms of – not revenge… punishment? – maybe we should call it 'treatment', but dealing with a child rather than a responsible adult is a different and more complicated problem. It seemed the most complex of the three scenarios so I decided to tackle that one.

The Latin paper was not as difficult as I had thought it might be. I stumbled on the Latin word 'dubitatio' which I didn't recognize. I translated it as 'dubious' but Pinky told me later it meant 'hesitation'.

After the exam, Pinky and I took the train down to Brighton, discussing the exam for the entirety of the journey. Our answers were similar but not the same, so there was a lot to discuss and loads to worry about.

I was to spend two weeks in Brighton, by the end of which the results of our exam might be received.

The Brighton Sanctum was far more modern than our own little 'shed' - wash my mouth out with soap! It was much bigger and had numerous desks, chairs and stools, and a well-equipped kitchen and store room.

It was immaculately clean, and unlike us, the Brighton Chapter employed a housekeeper which made working so much easier. The Brighton Chapter could get on with their work far more efficiently without spending an hour or two a day disinfecting the surfaces and jars and all the other ephemera we used day to day.

I was introduced to the Magister who was very welcoming, and invited me to a 'ceremony' which he was to conduct in the evening of the next day. I asked Pinky what a 'ceremony' was all about. He was cagey answering me. "Just a load of old waffle, really," he said, unreassuringly. "There's a lot of chanting and usually an evocation, but nothing to get excited about." Apparently, the Magister of Brighton liked to keep in touch with one or other of his spirit guides from time to time and would conduct these 'ceremonies' regularly.

"He might invite you to take part rather than just spectate," my friend told me. "Don't worry about it - it's quite harmless." Despite my friend's reassurances, I spent much of the day worrying about it.

Pinky gave me the grand tour of Brighton and we sat on the promenade eating an ice-cream. We played our 'Copy Cat Game' to a few unsuspecting souls – most notable was a boisterous teenager who was showing off to his friends. We followed him on to the pier and Pinky imitated his walk and gait perfectly. At the crucial moment, he had the lad trip and fall into a row of empty deck chairs. The lad limped away, cursing and swearing, blaming the deck chairs for being in the way.

"Don't you miss it?" my friend asked. "You know – family – a 'normal' life?" I said I had come to terms with distancing myself from such things. My life was 'normal' for me – maybe not to anyone else, but over the past six years of training, it was something I had come to accept.

"So, you don't mind it? I don't like the feeling of isolation," he said. I asked him to explain.

He had been to a family wedding – a cousin, I think - and said foremost he disliked not having a 'plus one' to take with him. He had considered taking a male friend with him, but thought that might give the wrong impression. "People do like adding two and two together to make five," he explained.

"Then there were those awful questions from well-meaning aunts and cousins – you know – where do you work? What do you do? Haven't you got a girlfriend? All those terrible questions for which we only have lies or half-truths as answers. It would've been so nice to say where I worked, what I was doing, what my ambitions were, who my friends were – you know – just normal things that most people would say."

I asked him if he doubted his vocation. "Not for a minute," he said. "I enjoy the work. It's challenging but interesting and I can't imagine myself doing anything other than this now."

As we talked, I realised I was not being honest – not only dishonest to my friend, but I was being untruthful to myself. "I do," I told him. "I do miss the 'normal life'. I'm resigned to being on my own throughout life, but it would be lovely to just lead an ordinary one – engage with family members, talk about your work to friends and acquaintances, have a wife and family of my own. It would be so easy to just forget everything I've learnt and go back to stacking shelves in the minimarket, chatting to customers and having a drink in the pub after work - having a chit-chat about the day I'd had. Yes - I miss that."

"What do you say, you and I have a right blow out before we end our novitiate? Let's go out there and give it one last blast of freedom! You know that if we become Adepts, our lives are going to change – we'll be far deeper into the Dark Arts and our responsibilities are going to multiply ten-fold."

I agreed. One last blow-out before we became Adepts seemed the right course of action. And this we did, starting there and then. "Come on," he said. "No talk of work – let's have some fun!" And we ran along the pier back to the promenade with not a clue where we were going to go or what we were going to actually do.

By eight that evening, we had somewhat run out of steam. After the tuppenny arcades, a fish and chip lunch on the seafront, several pints of beer and a ride on the rollercoaster at the end of the pier, we settled quietly into a little pub and talked about work. Work had become our lives – it had become all-consuming and we sat quite sullenly in the realisation that this was what our lives had come down to – two twenty-somethings, quietly supping ale talking about all the things we might have done, achieved or not achieved, had we taken different paths.

At eleven o'clock we were ready to retire for the evening and our great explosion of merry-making fizzled out like a faulty firework, never to be repeated.

The following day we tried to rekindle the energy we'd found the day before, but it didn't happen. We rambled around Brighton, visited little museums and moseyed around The Lanes not looking at or for anything in particular. We found an old herbalist near to The Lanes and spent a good couple of hours chatting with the shop owner, who was probably disappointed that for all the time we spent talking to him, he didn't make a sale.

It was a pleasant day and for me, at least, was spent in anticipation of the 'ceremony' we were to witness in the evening.

The 'ceremony' was conducted in a room in the Magister's own house. I had never seen inside my Magister's house – I wasn't exactly sure where my Magister lived. I was disappointed to see the Magister's house was just the same as any other house – a TV in the corner, a dining table and all the usual furnishings you might expect to see in any run-of-the-mill suburban home.

The room we were ushered into was plainly decorated with a mismatch of half a dozen or so chairs, a small card table (for want of a better description), a radiator and a threadbare rug. On the table was a candle on a candlestick, a small silver bell, two empty glasses and a black velvet pouch – the same as my Magister and I used for his 'special' potions. These pouches (I learned later) were purchased from Central Stores and were bought in bundles of ten or twenty, or a mixture of different sizes could be purchased at a premium. There was nothing 'special' about them at all.

Ridiculously, I had half expected the Magister to be dressed in a long flowing robe, but this was not the case. He was dressed in jeans and a t-shirt, and his assistant (who went by the name of Natalius) was similarly dressed, as was the fashion of the day in 1985.

'Pinky and I sat on the chairs provided, along with two other spectators whose identities I never got to know. The Magister emptied some water from a jug into the glass on the table. I thought there was some mystery to this, but soon realised that the water was there as the Magister's mouth became dry with all the chanting, so it was actually for his comfort and not for any esoteric usage.

The Magister chanted for an inordinate length of time. I recognised a lot of the Latin words and phrases he was using, but by and large it was gobbledegook. Natalius rang the bell from time to time, and wafted the candle about being careful not to extinguish it, protecting the flame with the palm of his left hand.

It seemed a long time before anything happened, and my backside was getting numb and uncomfortable on the hard chair. The Magister motioned for me to sit on the cushioned chair alongside the table in a friendly gesture. He did not speak to me directly.

As I sat down in the chair, he said a word 'hospite' [guest]. He repeated the word several times. He poured some water into the second glass and then poured the contents of the phial from the pouch into the water and lifted the glass, offering it to me to drink, which I did. The drink had a peculiar flavour – not like the sour flavour we made for querents but slightly sweet – like a strongly brewed cup of tea with just a granule of sugar.

He then looked at me directly and said the words 'Oculos tuo' - Close your eyes. I did as I was bid to do.

He continued to say 'hospite', repeatedly. I started to feel decidedly woozy, but I wasn't feeling faint or about to fall asleep. The best way I can describe how I felt was the sensation of having had a good drink and then laying down – it was that kind of swirling motion inside your head without the nausea. I guessed there had been something in the potion I had been administered, but I didn't feel unwell on any level, so continued as I was being asked to do.

The Magister then spoke to me directly again. "Continue to keep your eyes closed and relax. Nothing untoward is going to happen to you. Your senses have been awakened. A spirit wishes to commune with you." My senses of hearing and strangely of sight (seeing as I had my eyes closed) seemed to be sharper than usual. I had strong images coming into my eyes and the ringing of the bell went into my head and gave the sensation of reverberating.

"You need to give the spirit permission to commune with you. If you agree, say 'Assentior', if you wish to decline say 'Non assentior'. 'Assentior' or 'Non assentior'. Make your choice. I said as clearly as I could 'Assentior' – I had nothing to lose and potentially a lot to gain.

I now felt quite muzzy-headed. "The spirit will guide you," the Magister told me. "Be led and see what the spirit shows you. Do not try to manipulate what you see. Be led in what you see. The spirit wants to show you three images. Tell no-one what the spirit shows you. The images are a contract between you and the spirit. By agreeing to commune with the spirit, a contract between you has been made. The contract must not be broken."

Shapes and colours and misty wisps darted into my field of vision. The abstract forms began to gel together. An image came of my mother and of me as a young child – probably at three or four years of age. We were at the bedside of someone I was not familiar with – an old man with hardly any teeth and a broad smile. I stood beside the bed at head height to the man and my mother sat in a chair beside him. No words were spoken.

The man leaned over towards me and rested his hand on my head. He mouthed words, but I had no idea what he was saying or trying to say. We stayed in this image until it faded and the kaleidoscopic patterns took control again.

The abstract forms crossed my field of vision for a second time. The intangible shapes subsided. I could see myself sat where I was sitting next to the table. The ringing bell reverberated through my head. I was becoming disorientated.

My vision became blurred. When it cleared, I was being led towards the Archbishops Palace in Maidstone. We went through the front door to see the maze of corridors and stairs. I was whirled along corridors and upstairs and downstairs and out into the courtyard and then around again.

The image stopped abruptly. I could see no abstract shapes or images. There was a blackness. The word 'Pactum' [contract] came into view in burning letters.

A new picture swiftly presented itself. I was stood on a platform in a large auditorium facing rows of people sitting on hard-backed chairs. I couldn't fathom if this was a church or a meetings hall or what sort of building this was. I didn't recognise the place. The audience were sat there as though waiting for me to speak, but I did not know what it was I was supposed to tell them. The word 'Pactum' came in to view again and then dissipated into nothingness.

I felt a pressure through the temples on the side of my head – like a metal bar passing through them. The pain blinded me. I rubbed my temples to try to quell the soaring agony.

A voice came through the torturous pain – "Say 'Gratus sum tibi' [I am grateful to you]." I said the words and the pain subsided. I regained normal vision. "You have thanked the spirit for what he has shown you," the Magister said. I said the words again just to make sure the spirit had heard me. I needed to get rid of this agonising pain in my temples.

When I regained my normal sense, I had a strange feeling of being refreshed – oddly hydrated. I imagined that was probably how people feel after electric shock therapy. I did actually feel like I had been electrocuted and regained consciousness.

I had so many questions, but knew I could not retell what I had witnessed. I was hungry to know more. My Magister had showed me nothing akin to this and I was eager to learn as much as I could during my two weeks' stay in Brighton.

"I don't like Natalius much, to be very honest with you," Pinky told me as we strolled down to the seafront. "There's something a bit too dark about him – unsavoury. I keep him very much at arm's length. Don't get me wrong – he's done nothing wrong as far as I can see, but there's something that you might call 'dodgy' about him. You make up your own mind – don't take my word for it – it could just be me – I don't know what it is about him, I'm just wary, that's all."

I asked if he worked for the same Magister.

"Good God, no – he doesn't seem to be affiliated to anyone I know of."

We chatted for hours. I confessed that I was jealous of my friend's placement and that I would give my right arm to be working under his Magister.

"Careful what you wish for, my friend," he said, knocking me on my arm. I realised I had made a foolish and rash statement and one I would hopefully not come to regret.

My time in Brighton was at an end and our examination results had not come through yet. I said my goodbyes and took the bus back to Maidstone, changing at Tunbridge Wells half way.

As much as I missed the Brighton Chapter and my time spent there, it felt good to be in my own front door. Two envelopes were waiting for me on my doormat – the first from my Magister asking me to come in early on the Monday morning at eight as there was a special task he wished me to do. The second was my examination results. I had passed with a score of 96% and was informed that I would now be known as Peritus Liberius. I was to await further instructions.

Adept

Chapter 10

I got into work early on the Monday morning. I wanted to become familiar with what was happening with the workload prior to the Magister's arrival. The Magister had pre-empted me and was already in the Sanctum when I got there, muttering to himself.

He gave me a warm greeting and thanked me for getting to work ahead of time.

"Of course I want to hear all about your trip to Brighton," he said, "but we are somewhat pressed for time this morning. Tell me about it this afternoon. I've received a letter from the Magister of Brighton, by the way. I'll read it to you this afternoon. Are you alright?"

I told him I was fine and asked what the special assignment was that he needed me to perform.

"It's a bit of an odd one," he said. "You don't mind, do you?"

I said of course I didn't mind.

"Good," he said "bear with me. There is a house on St Lukes Avenue off Holland Road which is receiving some unwanted activity, well – the garden is, to be precise. I need you to investigate before I do anything further."

I asked what sort of activity and what information he needed.

"Goblins," he informed me.

"Goblins?" I asked.

"Yes, goblins," he said, "and don't pull a face like that. They do exist, you know?"

No, I didn't know. To be frank, I had no idea whatsoever.

"They're playing havoc with the vegetable patch," he told me. "The fairies are no match for them and they're causing all sorts of damage - uprooted vegetables, broken canes, all sorts of mischief. I need you to run up there and see what you can find."

"What am I looking for?" I asked, somewhat perplexed by the request.

"Bring me back any evidence of anarchy," he requested. "I have it in mind that Grobbleshank will be behind this. I've had problems with this particularly nasty little goblin before. See what you can find, will you? The householder is expecting you. Here – take this with you. Use this bag for gathering evidence. There are numerous pockets inside the bag where you can separate items from each other – we don't want any cross-contamination."

He handed me a bright pink shopping bag with little teddy bears attached to the side pockets. I looked inside the bag and indeed, there were multiple zipped pockets inside. Now, I'm not the type of man to have a macho persona, but truth be told, I wasn't altogether happy carrying this very effete bag all along the back of the prison wall, and along the full length of the very long Holland Road and then up the length of St Lukes Avenue.

"Be back by twelve, please?" he asked. "We need to be elsewhere by one."

I said I'd be as quick as I could be, and asked him to specify what it was he wanted me to salvage from the garden.

"Anything showing evidence of goblin activity," he said, "Grobbleshank in particular. The householder will be able to help you. Give him this note will you, please?" He handed me a sealed envelope.

I picked up the bag which I tucked under my arm to try to conceal it, and walked briskly up the Holland Road.

I arrived at my destination at about a quarter to nine and the householder answered the door to me. He was an affable fellow. I explained I was on an errand from my employer and he showed me round the back of the house to the garden. I handed him the sealed envelope. He read the note inside, then put it in his back trouser pocket. "Oh, I see," he said, not disclosing the contents of it.

He took me to the vegetable patch at the end of the garden. "It's here," he said. "Look!" and pointed to disrupted rows of parsnips and some uprooted Brussel sprout stalks. The damage was obvious, but I doubted this was goblin activity. It looked more like the work of a saboteur – maybe a neighbour he had fallen out with - but I took samples of the parsnips and a couple of Brussel sprout stalks.

"And look at this!" the householder took me to another area where some garden gnomes had been vandalised. "Look!" he said. "This one's lost his fishing rod and the head's come clean off this one!" He put the damaged gnomes into my bag.

I continued to look around the garden. There was a broken flower pot outside the shed door and then the householder pointed out a stone bird bath which had been emptied of water. I said to the house-holder that the bird bath was a little too big and heavy for me to take back with me in the bag. "What about this then?" he said, leading me over to a corner of the garden. Circles of stones looked like they had been disturbed recently. "My wife puts these out for the fairies," he said. "She's very upset. These are her fairy stones. They're supposed to be arranged in circles. This is more like a maze for them, which isn't acceptable at all. She thinks the fairies might not come back if they suspect Grobbleshank is the one causing the mischief."

I said I was sorry for his wife and that we would do what we could to help. He put half a dozen large stones in the bag which by now was getting weighty with the amount of evidence I had amassed. As much as I tried to conceal it, the head of one of the gnomes was protruding from the top of the bag.

I apologised for not being able to take the bird bath with me, and left the garden, lugging the bright pink shopping bag all the way back to the Sanctum. A couple of unruly teenagers teased me on the way, ribbing me about the shopping bag I was carrying. I could not repeat the words they chose to use in these pages - all I can say is that their insinuations were very much unfounded. I was back at the Sanctum by half past eleven, my arms aching with the weight of the bag.

"Ah, well done!" the Magister said as I put the heavy bag on his work bench. He looked through the bag and pulled out one of the damaged gnomes. "Shocking!" he said. "Absolutely shocking behaviour." He tut-tutted as he rummaged through the contents of the bag, pulling out a parsnip.

"I think I made a mistake," he said. "This isn't the work of Grobbleshank after all. This is the work of April Stultus!"

"Who is April Stultus?" I asked, naively.

"April Fool!" he said, creasing up with laughter, doubled up on the floor. I don't think I've ever seen someone laugh so long and so hard. He had tears rolling down his cheeks, clutching at his side.

"You are a wicked, wicked man," I said, also roaring with laughter, unable to see for the tears in my eyes.

"Grobbleshank!" he said through the laughter. "Grobbleshank!"

A knock on the door caused a temporary pause to our fits of giggles. It was the house-holder I had just met wanting to come in.

"Come in dear boy," the Magister said.

The man handed me the note which I had delivered to him earlier. It contained just three sentences – 'Make sure the bag is full to bursting. I don't want him tucking it under his arm on the way back. Remember to use the name Grobbleshank.'

I had been truly had - hook, line and sinker. All occupations play similar pranks on newcomers – the long weight in the hardware store, tartan breadcrumbs for Scotch eggs or asking at the perfumery if they had an ounce of scents. Our profession was no different.

I was introduced to the householder: "This is Peritus Ursinus," the Magister said. "Or, he was Peritus Ursinus, more strictly speaking." The householder had been the Magister's apprentice in his youth, but had left the profession to marry and to lead the so-called 'normal' life. They had kept in touch all these years later. What I didn't quite understand at the time was that the house-holder was well into his fifties, which begged the question – how old was the Magister exactly? The question had not crossed my mind before.

In the afternoon, after Peritus Ursinus had left and we had settled down, the Magister still let out a little chuckle every now and then. He asked me to sit down and took the letter from the Magister of Brighton out of his pocket. I was intrigued to know its content. The Magister read it out in full.

Dear Magister Honorius,

It has been my great pleasure to have played host to your Novitiate. He is a great credit to you.

I do know that my own Novitiate has benefited greatly from his visit. As we know, ours can be a lonely vocation - it can be a fillip to not feel entirely alone. Your Novitiate will be welcome here at any time.

I would like to inform you that your Novitiate shows enormous potential, and is a natural conduit for spiritualia of which you may not as yet be aware.

Your Novitiate has a clear mind and can demonstrate great focus. His is a natural ability which can be channelled and controlled at will. Restraint or limitation is not required.

If I can be of any service to you, I am, of course, your humble servant.

"What spiritualia is he referring to?" the Magister asked.

I told him about the first ceremony without filling in any of the details, but refrained from telling him about the second and third ceremonies the Magister of Brighton conducted on my behalf. He nodded. I was expecting to be reprimanded but instead he was encouraging.

"Well, then," he said, "there we have it. We'll work on a spirit guide for you. I have a certain spirit in mind who I know and trust, and if the Magister of Brighton has faith that you are ready, then so be it."

I asked the Magister if he had any idea what path Head Office had in mind for me.

"I don't know what Head Office has in mind for you, Peritus Liberius, but if you are happy to work alongside me in the meantime, I would be more than happy for you to do so.

I agreed. My life as an Adept had begun.

Chapter 11

I called round to see my mother. That isn't exactly true – I made an *appointment* to see my mother. Our relationship was no longer at a point of being able to 'drop in' - appointments and appointment lengths were pre-arranged. I agreed to see my mother between eleven and twelve on the Thursday. I had a burning question I needed an answer to.

The house had changed a lot since I had last been in there. It was newly decorated and my brother's bedroom had been turned into my mother's hobby room. She was a talented seamstress and her hobby room was filled with yarns and cloths and all manner of sewing paraphernalia.

My brother had moved in with his girlfriend, which was something else I didn't know. I expect I sound callous to say I really wasn't all that interested. I don't mean to be so cold-hearted, but I was losing touch with my mother and brother and any familial connection we had in the past.

"Is this just a social visit," she asked, "or do you want something?" Seems I wasn't the only one who was becoming uninterested.

"I want to ask you something, Mum," I said. "It's a bit weird, but I've been having this recurring dream and it's been bothering me."

"A dream? Are you serious? You've come to see me because of a dream? You've become weirder, as if that's possible."

"Sorry, Mum, but it's been troubling me and I don't know why." I was lying of course, but Mum wasn't to know that. I was getting better at distorting the truth undetected.

"Go on then, hit me with it – I'm getting my hair done at one and I don't want to be late."

"When I was little – did you take me to see an old man – a very old man, like he was on his death bed?"

"Well, there was Gerald, but you were far too young to remember him."

"Who was Gerald, Mum? Sorry to ask, but it's been playing on my mind."

"Gerald was my Godfather," she told me. "A strange old blighter if ever there was one. Lived up on the Mangravet Estate. He always looked out for me. He was a friend of my father's, I think. They used to work together – or else they met in the nick? I didn't think to ask. Why do you want to know?"

"I just keep on dreaming about him putting his hand on my head – like he was blessing me or something."

"I don't know why you'd be dreaming about that. You were only knee high to a grasshopper. Yes – he was dying – emphysema, I think. He'd been a chain-smoker for donkeys – didn't have two farthings to rub together. Mind you, for a man who didn't have anything much, he left ten bob in his will for you when he died. We opened your Post Office savings account with that. I never did know why he took such an interest in you – I mean, it wasn't as if we were related or anything."

"Did he say why he wanted to give me his blessing?" I asked.

"God only knows. Like I said he was a bit of a weirdo. Not the sort of person you'd want to meet in a dark alley. Mind you, he was always good to me. There's a box of his rubbish in the loft somewhere. Well, I suppose it's still there – I've never thrown it out anyway – just a load of old trinkets and his Bible. For all his faults he was a God-fearing man."

"Would you mind if I have a look?" I asked.

"Knock your socks off!" she said. "You'll need the steps – they're in the shed."

"Is there anything else you want from up there if I can get in?"

"Like what?"

"I've no idea, Mum."

"Well, don't be all day in there. I've got Maureen at one, remember."

I told her I'd be as quick as I could be. "Any idea what the box looks like?"

"Not a clue. It's not as if I'd remember a thing like that. God knows what you want it for!"

"By the way Mum," I said as I left the room to get the steps, "I've finished my apprenticeship."

"You've only just finished it? Good grief! That's taken you over six years – you must be slow!"

I ignored her snipe, got the steps and lifted myself into the attic space at the top of the stairs. In amongst the Christmas decorations, disused toys and boxes of junk, I found a small box marked 'Gerald'. As Mum had suggested, inside there were a few trinkets and half a dozen old dog-eared books. I took the box downstairs with me.

"I think I've found it," I said and showed Mum the box.

"That'll be it. Take it if you want it, but I can't think whatever for."

I thanked my mother and got ready to leave.

"Sit down a minute." My mother pointed to the settee, so I sat. This was an unusual move for her – in particular as she was having her hair done at one, and would probably get there half an hour before her appointment for a coffee and a gossip before her hour of pampering.

"I want to ask you something," she said. "What's with the ruby earring? I don't know what you think you look like - it makes you look a bit...peculiar."

I said it was a fashion thing – loads of blokes were wearing them.

She carried on. "Don't get upset, I just want to know. Are you gay? Only I was speaking with your brother and he says you're probably gay which is why you never talk about yourself. I mean, I don't care if you are, but it would be nice to at least know one way or another. Is the earring a gay thing?"

I told her I wasn't gay – I just hadn't found the right girl yet. She had no need to know of my occasional dalliances, and sad to say, if you – the reader of my journals – were hoping for some salacious gossip somewhere along the way, you will be cruelly disappointed. These pages are a memoir, not a confession.

"I hope you don't mind me asking. Only I always thought Gerald might've been gay, and now for some jumped up premise about a dream, you come here asking me about him. Like you, he never married. None of my business, I suppose. But anyway, if you say you're not, then I'll take that as gospel. And by the way, it wouldn't harm you to speak to your brother once in every blue moon. He won't go round yours – he says your place gives him the heebie-jeebies."

I said I'd try to keep in touch a bit better, but never did, of course.

I left my mother's house and went back to Peel Street, intrigued by the contents of the box I was carrying.

I made myself a cup of tea and sat down with the box to go through it.

If these were the treasures of Gerald's life, he didn't have much to show for it. As my mother had said, his Bible was in the box, along with a Timex watch which didn't work, a black bow tie, a silver-plated Christening spoon and four other books. The books were of some interest. The rest of his belongings could only be considered to be rubbish. I held on to them for a few weeks for the sake of respect, but eventually threw them away. They were no good to anybody and the man had been long dead.

The books, as I've said, were of some interest. There was a copy of Herman Hesse's Narziss and Goldmund, a book called Mental Poisoning – a Rosicrucian publication I had seen kicking about in the Sanctum at one time or another, another Herman Hesse book – Steppenwolf and a flea-bitten copy of John Donne's 'The Sun Rising'.

Gerald's orphic leanings were evident, but there was nothing in his possessions which indicated anything other than a passing interest in esotericism.

As a child, my academic leanings had started and finished with The Beano, looking at the pictures and seldom reading the narrative. I waded through the first chapter of Narziss and Goldmund almost to the second chapter, but the literacy level needed to read it were beyond my capabilities.

I put the books on my meagre bookshelf and not one of them saw the light of day again for a few years yet. An inscription in his Bible at least gave me Gerald's full name, but nothing else about the man came to light. I did ask the Magister if he had heard of Gerald, but that line of enquiry drew a blank. Why the spirit should have chosen the incident of being given the man's blessing is a mystery I had yet to solve. Sorry for the anti-climax.

Our work continued in the Sanctum. I was becoming more proficient in the mixing of potions, but still got quantities wrong – the ingredients were alright, but my measurements could be a bit 'off', much to the consternation of the Magister.

One such incident caused us no end of trouble and earned me a tut-tut from him – which in the Magister's world amounted to a well-rounded telling off.

A woman had contacted us who was experiencing difficulties in conceiving. Similar to a lot of women in the same predicament, all avenues of possible solutions had been exhausted. She saw us as pretty much her last resort. She had gone through the indignity of three phantom pregnancies and was at her wits' end. All she had ever wanted was to be a mother and nothing else would placate her.

Her husband, via questioning, was not as keen to become a parent as his wife was, and therein could have been part of the problem. His half-hearted efforts were not bearing fruit.

Following careful discussion with the Magister, we decided that a possible, although not infallible, solution would be to increase the husband's libido. The man was not impotent, but he lacked the enthusiasm required for the necessary...the necessary what? - the necessary 'conclusion'.

As usual, we did not disclose what our potential solution could be to our querents. As far as they were aware, we were helping to procure a conception. That was as much as they needed to know.

The Magister left the making of this potion in my hands. We did not want to draw attention to the husband's lack-lustre performance, so we instructed both querents to partake of the potion, thereby not apportioning blame to one or the other. The fancy phial and black velvet pouch came back into play again. We had started buying these in bulk. They are a handy bit of kit.

We had been able to purchase, via Central Stores, a drachm of ashwagandha. We already had at our disposal the other ingredients necessary for the potion. Ashwagandha is an Asian shrub not readily available in the UK, and I was not familiar with the correct dosage, but guessed the amount required. The symbol for the herb had no vertical lines so I considered it to be innocuous. Not being aware of all potentialities with the herb, I should have erred on the side of caution and increased or decreased the amount administered, depending on the drug's potency. I omitted to follow this simple instruction and went full out with maximum dosage.

The affects the potion had were two-fold. As planned, the husband's appetite for his carnal urges improved dramatically, but the wife's interest dropped distinctly. Her anxiety about her situation fell off the scale, leaving the husband with 'unfulfilled potential', for want of a better expression.

The state of affairs between the couple had become untenable. Each blamed the other - thankfully neither of the two thought we (or our potion) had been the problem.

I did adjust the dosage and tweaked the ingredient quantities, creating two potions, one for him and one for her, so no lasting harm was done.

I would like to report that the revamped potions had the desired effect, but I am going to disappoint you for a second time. The couple separated. Whether or not the woman's dreams were eventually realised, I am not able to divulge - we received no further communication from her.

I received my 'virtual smack on the wrist' from the Magister and ate nothing but humble pie for a fortnight.

Facilis Descensus Averno.

Chapter 12

Two months following being promoted to Adept, I was still waiting to hear from Head Office about a potential project I could work on.

I was really hoping I would be asked to relocate to Brighton, and I would check the mail delivery every morning to see if my wish was to be fulfilled.

"I've been reviewing your performance," my Magister said, "and following on from the letter I received from the Magister of Brighton, I think it's time to start thinking about organising a spirit guide for you. Will you be OK with that?"

I said I felt ready for it, but underplayed my keenness to pursue this angle of work.

"Good then, I'll arrange it," he said. "We need a blank room – I'll make some enquiries."

I asked why we needed a 'blank' room and what that meant exactly.

"We need a space with limited furnishings and no other ephemera."

I asked why the room had to be so bare.

"They get easily distracted – the spirits do. It's best to operate in any empty room, but we still need chairs and a table. I don't think my back would take standing for a long period of time. Otherwise, we could have done without the chairs. Apart from that, it's better the room's empty."

I said that what he had said made sense. He had not mentioned that he had been experiencing back problems previously. In fact, he didn't really talk about his health at all, but like all people of a certain age, he most probably did have some health concerns. It just hadn't occurred to me before now.

"I know someone in the Planning Department in County Hall – there are loads of empty rooms there. That would be our best bet. I'll nip down this afternoon and see what he can do for us."

I asked him what the potion might have been which I was administered in Brighton.

"It would have been a mild hallucinogen," he told me. "Probably a weak infusion of magic mushrooms. Harvested on a new moon, the mushrooms only have a negligible effect. Some practitioners use a stronger solution, such as that produced from mushrooms harvested on a full moon, and some even take illicit drugs to attain a deeper or more detailed phantasm, but these should only be used if strictly necessary and under caution. People have been known to become addicted to not only the drug but the experience with alarming speed. I wouldn't advise it – one's grip on reality can be permanently damaged."

Facilis descensus averno. I took heed of the warning.

The Magister continued. "As you know, spirits are part of this world, but only exist on a spiritual not a physical plane. They can communicate with us and can interact with us but as much as they are part of our world, we must remember that we exist on a physical, tangible plane. We cannot exist on a purely spiritual level. Some people make the mistake of trying to transcend our physical existence to become part of the spiritual plane, which is not possible. Let me put it like this – as much as you might love dogs and admire them and love to interact with them, no matter how deep your affiliation is with dogs, you cannot for any amount of trying, become a dog. This fixation with spiritualia is when things can go very badly wrong. Some practitioners become obsessed and the obsession can only lead to disappointment and psychosis. Bear this in mind, please - never allow spiritualia to become more important than our tangible reality. Therein lies the beginning of madness."

It was rare to hear the Magister speak so deeply. He spoke earnestly and with feeling. He was doing his very best to keep me safe and I appreciated his sentiment.

"What is it a spirit wants?" I asked. "What motivates a spirit to assist us? What do they want to get out of our interaction?"

"Good question," the Magister answered. "In the physical world we have driving forces – sex, money, security, survival, leisure and so on. The mark of a man is defined by the force driving him. Spirits also have their own ambitions, be it mischief, creation of chaos or whatever. Their primary motivation is power – they want influence, authority, supremacy and control. Power is all-encompassing for them. They are highly competitive and vie for position and sovereignty. An over-ambitious spirit becomes dangerous – they will lie and deceive to achieve their desire."

I was glad I had asked the question.

The Magister suggested he would try and secure a little room at County Hall for Friday afternoon.

"Friday afternoon is a good time to do this," he informed me. "A lot of the staff at County Hall finish early on a Friday, so the building will be largely empty and there should be no likelihood of us being disturbed. I've got a friend who works there – he should be able to find something suitable for us."

He continued to explain what he intended to do. "I will introduce you to a spirit guide I use from time to time. The spirit will be able to recommend a suitable guide for you. Make a note of a couple of questions you might like to ask your spirit. Form a mental image of what it is you want to know – the spirit will understand. Try not to ask anything too specific and definitely nothing which might require a yes or no answer. Be prepared for lies. If the spirit isn't happy with the question you ask, more likely than not they'll make something up. They don't like to appear to not know the answer to something. It's a power thing with them."

I had too many questions to narrow it down to just a couple. I practiced conjuring up the images in my mind. This was all very new to me and it would take a while before I mastered the questioning.

"What is the purpose of the bell?" I had seen the bell previously and guessed it was something to do with evoking spirits.

"The bell is to 'ground' you, so to speak. It can stop you from drifting too far into the spirit world – it can bring you back into reality. It doesn't have to be a bell – it could be a klaxon if you so wished, but a bell is a bit kinder on the eardrum, don't you think?"

I asked why a bell is used in a Catholic Mass. That (and incense) always seemed a bit odd to me.

"Organised religion is not something we would normally discuss, as you well know. But in a Mass, the ringing of the bell is supposed to mark the exact time the bread and wine become flesh and blood. I'm sorry if that doesn't make any sense to you, but it doesn't to me, either. As I understand it, incense is a symbol of purification or prayers rising up to God. I think the use of it is more historical, dissipating the stench of the great unwashed. Is there anything else you want to know just now? If not, I'll nip down to County Hall and try and book us a room."

I said I'd think about it. He reminded me to think about questions I would like to ask. If I had have had a bit more time, I wanted to ask about the Magister's spirit guide or guides, but it was too late. He plopped his Trilby on his head and he was out the door.

I don't know why I was so fixated about it, but I really wanted to know more about Gerald. It seemed so odd to give such a young child he barely knew his blessing. It didn't really matter as Gerald was long gone, but I wanted closure to it.

I knew that if I asked something about the future a spirit wouldn't be able to tell me – well, they would but it would be at best a guess, but I wanted to know which path was going to suit me best. That is a round-about way of asking the same thing, but I might get some sort of an intelligent answer.

I continued to think about my questions and how best I could ask them, and continued with the work I had started earlier.

The Magister arrived back at about four, which was a long time for a walk to County Hall. "Couldn't get it," he said." It seems my friend no longer works there. I got us a room in the Archbishops Palace, though, but it wasn't cheap. Ah well, seeds thrust where the weevil thrives."

I loved his use of silly plays on words – that and the little poems he'd come out with. If I was chatting too much and not concentrating on my work, he'd say.

A friend I once had made a racket,

In the end I just couldn't hack it.

When he opened his gob,

My eardrums would throb

And I was near to old hell as God damn it!

He always spoke in jest, but I'd quieten down, taking the hint.

The room was booked for three hours on the Friday afternoon, which the Magister said would give us plenty of time. He showed me the recipe for the evocation potion. The forthcoming ceremony (although he didn't call it a ceremony, instead calling it a 'ritual') was no longer discussed. I did try to ask him for more information and he just answered with the word 'Friday' and we'd get on with our work.

The day prior to the 'ritual', he sent me on my own to assess a case. This was the first time I had been allowed to go singly, and I felt rather honored that he trusted me enough to allow it.

"You can meet the client in his shop," he told me. "I don't know if there's anything we can do to help - I only know some sketchy details. Perhaps you could gather some more detailed information. Don't promise anything to the trader, but get the info and we'll see what we can do. He'll be expecting you." He pulled my head gently to one side. "Good, you've got your earring in. Off you go then."

I agreed to go and took a notebook and pen with me.

"It's bloody killed it off, that bloody Stoneborough Centre has. Used to be thriving round here – now look!" The greengrocer waved at the street outside from his chair behind the counter. "Dead as a proverbial," he said. "They're all packing up down here," he continued. "See 'im – 'im over there – been 'ere for three generations he has, now look, not a soul in 'is shop." He pointed to a butcher's shop across the way. "We can't compete no more," he said, "not at their prices." (I assumed he was talking about the shops in the Stoneborough Centre). "There ain't nuffink we can do about it. That's why I called you lot in. I don't know who else to ask. Is there anyfing you can do? I mean – I'll pay yer."

I took down some details about the lack of footfall, where his sales used to be and where they were now. "Thing is," he said, "greengrocers ain't like other shops – our stuff goes off real quick. If you ain't got the turnover it all goes manky right smartish." He held up a brown and soggy lettuce to make his point.

I had actually been to school with the man's son, but I didn't tell him that, of course.

"Yes, love," he said to a woman who had come in to the shop, speaking from his chair behind the counter. She picked up an onion and smelled it. "Fresh in this morning, those are love. You won't get nothing as fresh as that in the supermarket." I doubted his honesty. You could see the onions in the stack were not looking their best – some had started to sprout.

"I think I'll leave it, thank you," the woman said smiling, leaving the shop.

"I can do you a good price on yer Jersey Royals," he called out after her. She turned and smiled and continued along the pavement.

I took a gentle stroll back to the Sanctum. I noted the closed-up shops and the lack of life in the once bustling Week Street.

The town centre was dying and it seemed like a bleakness – an austerity - was wreaking havoc wherever you looked. A death-knell was ringing throughout the place.

I got back to the Sanctum and there was a note left on my work station – 'Back bad. Doctor's appointment. See you in the morning. Write up your findings, please.'

It was unusual for the Magister to leave such a note. I had a terrible foreboding that all was not well with him.

Chapter 13

We made our way down to the Archbishops Palace for one o'clock. We walked at a slow pace, the Magister making use of an old walking stick. He winced on occasion when climbing up or down a pavement. The man was obviously in pain. Other than the grunting noises he made, he did not complain.

We arrived at the Palace at about ten to one. He told the lady at the front desk that he had reserved a room and was directed to go to one of the attic rooms, which were usually used for children's music lessons. The wails of some child massacring Fauré's Requiem on a viola greeted us as we ascended the steep stairs into the attic. I sound educated, don't I? The Magister told me what the music and instrument were. The room was surprisingly sound-proofed when I closed the door.

It was empty except for two chairs, an upright piano and a music stand. How anyone had managed to get the piano up those stairs defied logic. The Magister folded up the music stand, put it on top of the piano, got a black sheet out of his briefcase and covered the piano with it. On top of that he put a simple white candle in a holder and placed a small silver bell to the side of it.

"Draw those curtains, can you please?" he asked as he lit the candle. I did as I was bid.

"I have to ask," he said, "but we're going to be here a couple of hours. Do you need the toilet before we begin? It's on the ground floor if you do."

I told him I didn't and he motioned me to sit on one of the chairs. He took a glass, a thermos flask (containing water) and the elixir (as he called it) out of his case, and put them on the top of the covered piano.

"Ready?" he asked. I was ready.

"Spiritus te ipsum praedicat!" he chanted − 'Spirit declare yourself!' He motioned for me to join in.

"Spiritus te ipsum praedicat! Spiritus te ipsum praedicat!" The candle flickered.

"We have company!" the Magister announced, as the candle flickered. "Best take the elixir now." I did as suggested.

"Concentrate on the images which come to you," the Magister said. "I'm questionning the spirit on your behalf for the time being. This spirit's name is Gregor, by the way. He is one of my spirit guides. I am asking him if he can suggest a spirit guide for you. As expected, he is suggesting himself – power hungry as he is. Continue to concentrate."

The Magister rang the bell. "Another spirit is trying to usurp power here," the Magister told me. "He is resident here and is trying to assert his authority. Abite Spiritum! Abite Spiritum!"

A breeze passed over me. "Abite Spiritum! Spirit be gone!"

I saw all sorts of images – not just the shapes and colours like I had seen before. A darkness was pervading my field of vision. The Magister rang the bell. "Keep grounded. I need to eject this spirit – he's mischief." He rang the bell again. "The spirit is trying to state his dominance. He is saying he has jurisprudence in this place and does not recognise my authority. He's a nuisance."

An image fell slap-bang in the middle of my optical axis. A door opened in front of me – I was being led through it in a hurry. To the left of me was a hollow in a rock. I suppose you could call it a 'cave' but it did not give the general appearance of a cave – just an entrance.

"Follow the spirit that guides you," the Magister said. "I'll deal with this menace."

I stayed in the place to which I had been led. The bell sounded in my head reminding me I was still in the physical world. A raised index finger was raised in front of me. I knew to stay where I was – it was a signal you might give to a dog to 'Stay!'

The image of the finger dissolved into the blackness. All was dark. I could hear the bell but see nothing. Incrementally, a light appeared in the distance. I remained still – the light edged towards me and then suddenly – like a flash – I was in a beautiful garden. I was transported towards a shed in the corner of the garden and the door opened for me.

Inside the shed was a table and on it was a Bible, Gerald's Bible. I could see the inscription to him on the front page. The pages flipped open resting on a verse with which I was unfamiliar. The verse came from the book of Proverbs: 'He that walketh with wise men shall be wise: but a companion of fools shall be destroyed.'

Next to the Bible was a letter which I was unable to read, and a ten-shilling note.

The pages of a second book turned over. Another quotation came into focus - this time from Hesse's Narziss and Goldmund: '...put myself in the place in which I am best able to serve...'

This didn't seem to be about Gerald, although the passage marked was similarly marked in the copy I had found (which I checked later).

My interest became more aroused at the third and final quotation, this time from Hermann Hesse's Steppenwolf. The pages flipped over and over and over again, pausing in between turning. The name 'Harry' was highlighted whenever it appeared.

My guide's name was Harry. Harry took me to the window of the shed and I looked out on to the beautiful garden. Harry had given me some answers about Gerald, or at least had made reference to him. I had yet to ask about a path for me. I conjured the image of the crossroads I had practiced previously and a mist formed across the window, obscuring the garden.

The mist faded and a picture of a church came before me. Of all things I had expected to see, a church did not even make the list. I have never been, nor am I now, interested in organized religion. Why give me the image of a church?

I heard the bell ring and the Magister calling to me. "Time to go, time to go."

I came out of my stupor to find the Magister looking intently into my eyes. "Tell me on the way back," he said and put the candle, bell, glass, phial and cloth back into his case. "Open the curtains will you, please?" I obeyed, of course.

"You're looking troubled," he said as he limped back to the Sanctum.

"I've seen things I really don't understand," I said. I understood the quotations vaguely, but the image of the church made no sense at all.

"And your spirit guide?" he asked.

"I think it's 'Harry'," I answered.

"Yes, yes," he said. "I thought it might be. I've had cause to meet Harry myself at times. Nice chap – you can't go wrong there."

I asked what happened with the mischievous spirit. "Bastard thing wouldn't leave us alone, a right pain in the arse!" the Magister told me. "I had to get heavy-handed in the end."

"Heavy-handed how?" I asked, surprised by the Magister's use of bad language.

"There are spirits way above him in the pecking order. I had to call one of those in the end – not a thing I do lightly. By the way," he continued, "have you given any thought to the greengrocer's problem?"

"I don't see there's a lot we can do," I said. "I think it's more of a marketing problem than anything else. He sits behind his counter on his little chair, and you feel you're disturbing him by asking for something. It would be better if he sat on a high stool – I understand it would be very wearing to stand all day, but at least customers could see him. If he were to stand up when they came in, he could appear to be a bit more welcoming."

"Yes, indeed," the Magister agreed. "Anything else?"

"I think if the customers are not coming to him, then perhaps he could go to the customers."

"How do you mean?"

"Well," I said, "in the sixties and early seventies, we had teams of people delivering things in vans – greengrocery, bakery, the coal man, fizzy drinks – they all came to us – it wasn't worth getting a bus in to town just to get a couple of things, in particular heavy things. If he took the greengrocery to big estates such as Ringlestone, Shepway or Mangravet - I'm sure he'd have a very grateful and eager clientele."

"Good thinking," the Magister said. "Propose that to him – see how he feels about it. Perhaps he could diversify a bit as well, selling other heavy groceries. Thinking off the top of my head here, but things like washing powder are a nuisance to lug back from town. Suggest that as well. Perhaps we ought to get a payment for our troubles, though. Perhaps offer him an incantation he can use to drum up trade."

"What sort of incantation?" I asked,

"Oh, I don't know – gobbledegook. Set him a dissonant course of action – I'm sure you can come up with something appropriate – you seem to have a gift for creating nonsense."

Indeed, I could and I did. The greengrocer got some very funny looks standing on two empty vegetable crates outside on the pavement. I told him to chant 'venient in placere' [come in, please] whenever there were no customers in his shop. Curiosity alone brought customers in. Problem solved - as the Magister would say, 'after a fashion'.

The greengrocer's son took on the veg round in their clapped-out van, the father staying on in the shop. I couldn't help but feel this was a stay of execution rather than a reprieve for the shop and the town centre.

I did not have the inclination to question my mother further about a possible letter she might have received from Gerald along with the ten shillings, so I let that sleeping dog lie.

Chapter 14

The Magister was taken into hospital. He wouldn't say the reason for his treatment and the nurses and doctors weren't forthcoming, either. I did learn that he had nominated me as next of kin, but apart from that, I knew nothing.

"Don't worry about me," he said. "Just focus on what you're doing while I'm away. I'll be back on my feet soon enough."

He wasn't. I continued with our work and learnt a lot at that time having to work out things for myself. I visited the Magister as often as practicable, but being in the new Maidstone Hospital, it meant a bus ride rather than a quick two-step up to the West Kent Hospital in Marsham Street.

A week into the Magister's stay in hospital, the long-awaited notification from Head Office arrived. The letter congratulated me on my recent examination pass, and asked me to phone the Head Office administrator to discuss a potential project which could be of interest to me.

Naturally, I rang at my first opportunity. The project they advised I could assist with was centred on this: a protestant church in an East London borough (which I am unable to name for this record) had been experiencing some problems, and the vicar of the church had requested some help. Should I accept the task, I would be housed in nearby bed and breakfast accommodation, all meals and travel expenses paid for (receipts required) and the vicar would allow me use of his vestry. The nature of the 'problem' was not disclosed. If I was in agreement, I was asked to take the train from Maidstone East Station on the following Monday morning.

I took the bus to the hospital to discuss this proposal with the Magister.

"I can't see any reason why you shouldn't take the task," he advised. "If they thought the problem beyond your capabilities, they wouldn't have suggested that you would be a suitable candidate. We've nothing pressing or that won't wait. Take it – the change might do you good."

I called the administrator back and said that I was up for the challenge. I asked if there was anything I needed to take with me and they suggested a few clothes as I could be a while, other than that - nothing. No timescale had been put on the task, but if I needed more changes of clothing or anything from the Sanctum, they would pay for me to nip back to Maidstone to get it.

I had doubts whether I was the right candidate for this. My knowledge of church matters was seriously lacking. However, I had nothing to lose and I duly arrived at Charing Cross Station at around eleven, with a suitcase of clothes and a few compounds and vessels I thought might be appropriate. I had never been to London before - a helpful ticket master helped me to navigate my way around the London Underground.

///

I arrived at my destination. It was a modern-built Anglican church, with steep steps leading up to the front door. I went inside and knocked on the vestry door. The vicar greeted me and we sat in the vestry with a welcome coffee and chatted about the parish I was being asked to help.

East London was something of a shock to me. Maidstone was not without its problems and its poverty –but East London was a different animal altogether. It was a diverse community, which the church to which I had been assigned coped with admirably. They laid on a plethora of community projects, embracing all creeds and beliefs.

"We believe everyone is entitled to their own beliefs – we're not trying to force anything down anyone's throat or convert anyone," the vicar told me. "Everyone is welcome – we are a community more than we are a Church – rather than preach, we try to integrate and assist."

I admired his community spirit. The vicar was about forty and chose not to wear a dog-collar. "I think a dog-collar tends to set one apart and can make one look aloof – above other people. I'm very much a part of this community, and I like the locals to look at me as someone who can help them rather than look down on them from some lofty pedestal."

This man was refreshingly down to Earth with no 'holier-than-thou' attitude. I liked the man. I just wondered what he might make of me.

In a friendly way, he asked me about myself. He understood that by the very nature of my work I was unable to fill in all the details for him. It would have been nice to have been as open and candid as he was, but he accepted the restraints put upon me by the nature of my profession.

I was still waiting to know what the task was that I was being asked to address.

"There is an element creeping into this parish which we – that is, the Church – are none too happy about. We are at a loss as to how to deal with the situation, let alone know how to combat it with any effectiveness. In recent months, I have been contacted by six or seven parishioners – only one of them an actual member of my congregation, who claim that they are being cursed. They believe they had had hexes put on them by a person or persons unknown. I spoke to a Catholic priest friend of mine – he said he had used your organisation for something or other some years back, and put me in touch with you. I'm not expecting miracles, but I just hope that you are able to help in some way."

I said I would do what I could and asked him the nature of the jinxes his parishioners were experiencing.

"I'm no authority on such matters," he explained, "but these seem to be voodoo, or as some call it around here, 'ju-ju'. All those who have come to me have found effigies of themselves in some form or another and are living in total fear."

I asked if this was a recent trend or had it been practised in the area for a while.

"I'm afraid I really couldn't tell you. Such things go on behind closed doors. Those I've spoken to are very cagey about giving me any specific details."

"Would I be able to talk to any of these victims?" I asked him.

"Most certainly you can – I'm glad you've asked me. Can I ask you though – man to man – do you believe in this voodoo business yourself? I understand if you can't tell me, but I would like to know."

I told him I was not affiliated to any organised religion. I went on to explain that voodoo was a very powerful belief system. The voodoo priests or priestesses do not have any power in themselves. The only influence they have is to make people believe that they have a power of some kind. There is no power in the effigies themselves, only in the belief that the effigies convey power.

I continued: "Belief is a very powerful thing. As I understand it, in your religion, belief can achieve almost anything - including the power to heal."

"Indeed, we do. We lay hands on the sick – but it is not the laying on of hands which can heal – it is the belief that the laying on of hands heals. This is where the sufferer becomes unstuck – they think it's the action of the laying on of hands which could cure them and not the belief in the possibility."

We continued to discuss the power of belief well into the early evening, when he suggested we go to a restaurant which was en route to my B & B.

Over dinner I told him about the power of dissonance, and said that after I had spoken to his victims, I would be best placed to offer some sort of a solution to the problem.

"The problem we face," I went on to say, "is that we need to destroy the belief in the thing that is troubling them. Remove the belief and the problem is solved."

"Have you ever thought of taking up the cloth?" the vicar asked me as we left the restaurant. "You give a much better sermon than I ever could. You're a natural."

We laughed and I said that I was in the business of putting order into chaos - I would hate to create more chaos by threatening people with eternal damnation. He roared with laughter and we arranged to meet in the vestry of the church the next morning at ten. He turned back for a moment.

"You're a credit to your profession," he said. I told him I hadn't done anything yet and he laughed again, walking away.

Only one person turned up for me to consult with the following morning. He was a man in his mid-twenties who looked very nervous. I tried to put him at ease. I told him I was not connected to the church and that anything he told me was totally confidential. He was not a member of the vicar's congregation and I suggested that perhaps we could sit outside, hoping that not being in the church would put him more at ease.

He agreed, and we found a nice quiet corner on a bench outside.

"You're not an exorcist, are you?" he asked me.

I assured him I was no such thing.

"What are you then?" I told him I simply put order into chaos. He said he understood, but I could see in his face he understood diddly-squat.

"Tell me in your own words what has happened," I said, "and tell me how you feel about it now."

He didn't know who had put the curse on him. I told him it was usually someone a victim knows, as the effigy would have something personal attached to it. I asked him what that was. He drew the doll out of his jacket pocket. It was a crude affair which had no affinity to the man sat beside me. A lock of hair was pinned to the figure, the pin penetrating an eye. The effigy had been posted through his letterbox.

I asked him where the lock of hair could have come from – or how it might have been collected, if indeed it was his?

He said he didn't know – he had no enemies as far as he knew, but had had a row with a neighbour a few weeks back. It was only a minor argument and he conceded to allow the neighbour use of his driveway as he didn't need it himself, in return for the neighbour keeping the area clear of weeds.

I asked how the neighbour might have got a lock of his hair, if the perpetrator was his neighbour. He could think of no opportunity the neighbour could have had to have done so and believed the falling out to have been resolved.

I also asked him if he knew where the local voodoo temple was located. He said he didn't, but I could tell by his reaction that he was too frightened to tell me. He had that ocular appearance of a 'rabbit caught in the head-lights'. I remember my brother having the self-same expression when Mum found out he'd been suspended from school for putting a slow worm in the school Secretary's handbag.

I paused, but the man refused to tell me where the temple might be. "And how do you feel at this point in time?" I asked him. "Does your eye hurt? Do you have a pain in your eye? How are you feeling?"

He said he was experiencing no pain, but his eye had become blurry. I could tell that he was living in fear. I suggested removing the pin and the hair, which he refused to do.

I left him with the question of who he thought could have been responsible for this, and instructed him to remove just one hair from the doll each day.

He agreed to do that and we agreed to meet up in a week's time. "Meanwhile," I said, "do me a favour and have your eyes checked at the optician's." At this time, this was a free National Health service, so the man had nothing to lose. He agreed.

When we had finished our consultation, I went back into the vestry and spoke with the vicar. "What do you think?" he asked me.

"The man is obviously terrified that something bad is going to happen to him," I said. "Convincing him otherwise is not going to be easy. He showed me a doll with hair attached to it, but the hair had a grey tinge to it – I don't think it was his." I told him what I had instructed the man to do.

"I hope you don't mind me asking, but what do you think of this one?" the vicar said, handing me a typed document.

The letter was from a colleague of his, not from the same parish. He had read the letter a fortnight ago, but was unsure how to respond to it. It read something along the lines of the following:

'I have been contacted by one of my parishioners who believes himself to be the target of a curse. Some years ago, the man – a plumber, now in his fifties – fell foul of a gypsy woman who accosted him while on holiday in Benidorm. The woman was blocking his path, trying to sell him a small bunch of lavender. "It will bring you good luck!" the woman told him, but he was having none of it and tried to push past her. Several other women surrounded him, shouting and calling him an English pig. As he tried to get through the group, one of the women fell to the ground, as though shoved. The man swears blind he didn't knock her over, yet the confrontation with the women escalated. They spat on him, chanting 'English pig! English pig! English pig!' and it wasn't until the intervention of Spanish police ended the skirmish. He was led away to safety and the woman who first accosted him called out to him – "English pig, act like a pig, you become a pig" and spat on the ground at his feet. The police took him out of harm's way as the women continued to scream out after him.

'It was some months later, having shelved the episode into an after-dinner anecdote, that he overheard a couple of men, who were not familiar with the account of the incident, talking about him as a recommended plumber – not in any derogatory way, but using a nickname he hadn't heard before. His surname was of East European descent, and was generally pronounced as 'Gillespie' although it was not spelled or correctly pronounced that way. The men referred to him as 'Piggy Gillespie', akin to the name of the jazz musician, Dizzy Gillespie. He confronted the men who said they meant no harm – it was just what they had heard other people calling him the same thing, and assumed it was his usual nickname. At that point, he hadn't attributed the name-calling to the gypsy woman's curse – 'you become a pig'.

'The man had put on something of a summer party for his grandchildren with a paddling pool and a barbecue, and several of his grandchildren's friends had come to join in the fun. As children do, they were larking about, thoroughly enjoying splashing in the water, squealing and generally running amok.

One of the grandchildren's friends said to his friend "Your grandad looks like a pig – a piggy-pig-pig". Children being children, the other's joined in the name-calling, until they were all saying it.

The man became distraught that the gypsy woman's curse seemed to have been realised. He is asking how the curse can be reversed? It wouldn't be possible to find the woman who had put the curse on him. Please help.'

"It certainly is an odd one," I told the vicar. I said that I had dealt with and removed a few curses previously. Most are simple matters of belief – like the voodoo curses they were trying to resolve now. I said I would sleep on it. Perhaps it would be a good idea to contact his friend who had sent him the letter and tell him that he had asked a friend for his advice and that he would get back to him as soon as he could, and to please pass on this message to the complainant.

My feeling was that if the man came to believe that something was being done about the situation, he was more likely to believe that the curse could be lifted and hence solved.

The vicar and I chatted into the late hours of the evening, both of us learning much about the other. It occurred to me that our paths were not as different as they would first appear to be.

Chapter 15

That week I met two other victims of the voodoo cursing. Their experiences were much the same as the first sufferer – an effigy had been posted through their letterboxes and they were unsure who the perpetrator could be. It seemed to me that this was not the work of a voodoo priest or priestess, but was from someone who was seeking power over the cursed, and their plan was working. Someone was taking great amusement from the suffering of others. We (the vicar and I) needed to isolate the perpetrator for this to stop – or it would only get worse.

Thorough questioning of the victims revealed a connection between them – a local hairdresser. They all visited the same salon. In conversation with the hairdresser, as well as their forthcoming holiday arrangements, they talked about their ailments and other details of their lives. The hairdresser probably enjoyed hearing about the problems they were experiencing and relished listening to their fears knowing that he was the perpetrator.

I discussed my suspicions with the vicar and made some suggestions. Firstly, the victims needed to feel protected from the threats which had been presented to them, and the vicar was in a privileged position to help with that. I asked if he actually had a dog collar to wear, and he said he did have one but seldom wore it. I also asked if he had the other vestments relevant to his profession and he told me there were some in the vicarage left behind by the previous occupant. I asked him to dig these out. "We need to be able to give the victims reassurance," I said. "Just being a man of the cloth is not sufficient in this situation. We have to instil faith in your abilities as a vessel of the Church."

I asked him if he had any learning in respect of Latin. "Good Lord, no," he admitted. "We haven't used Latin in a protestant church for generations."

I explained the psychology of using Latin on the general populace. "People believe there is a special power in using Latin for ceremonies. Of course, we know it to be nonsense, but the use of Latin as well as the use of water (baptisms, Christenings, etc) are a crucial element in persuading people that something special is being orchestrated." I asked him if he was able to learn the Lord's Prayer in Latin – maybe with the help of the local library. If not, I could send him a copy of it.

"Your pronunciation doesn't matter," I told him. "No-one would know if you say the words correctly or incorrectly. You could just say a load of old Latin phrases, but they might be recognised. Best to use something not recognisable but have it sound authentic. There is a rhythm to the Lord's Prayer which makes it recognisable in any language – especially if recited in a slow, low tone."

I described the notion of the dissonance I had in mind. "I think you should wear full vestments – or as many as you can muster. Tell the victim you are going to protect them from any incoming evil – tell them that God will protect them. Have them kneel in front of you – it's a gesture of submission to authority. Use English to say words to the effect of 'Heavenly Father, protect your child from the evil as presented to him (or her). Surround him with your love and shelter him from the wicked.' You'll be better at coining the right phrases. Hold your right hand above their head as they kneel. I'll give you a special glass phial which you should just fill with any old water. Holy water - if you believe there is any power in it. It doesn't matter. Say words like 'May the holy power of this blessed water purify and protect' and make the sign of the cross on their forehead with a drop of the water. Now for the *pièce de résistance* – the grand finale. Continue to hold your hand above their head and then recite your well-rehearsed Lord's Prayer in Latin. Do you think you could manage all that? Oh, I'll need their effigies back, please. Waft the effigies about in the flame of a large white candle and say words like 'With the power vested in me as a vessel of Christ on Earth, I extinguish any malevolent purpose'. Place emphasis on the word 'extinguish' and place the effigy under the cross on the altar and leave it there. Have you got all that?"

He said he understood and asked if this was a bit deceitful?

"The end justifies the means," I told him. "You do christenings, don't you? You don't get much more deceptive than that." He agreed and laughed. "Remember please, I need those effigies. Someone is going to get a taste of their own medicine. I'll give you a call in a week or so and see how you get on. I'll come back when you have the effigies."

He said he'd let me know, then said "I think I'm going to miss you when you're gone. It's been great working with you."

I said I'd be with him in spirit. "Quite literally, if you don't behave," I said. He laughed raucously.

"Oh, sorry, one other thing," the vicar asked. "Have you had chance to think about the letter we discussed – the man who believed he was turning into a pig?"

"Ah, yes, sorry – nearly forgot. If someone came to you distressed that he was going bald, would you suggest the laying on of hands, or praying and fasting?"

"No, of course not," he replied. "It's hereditary, isn't it? No amount of prayer could reverse that."

I told him he was right, there would be nothing I could do, either. "I could give the man a potion, but that would be true deceit and not ethical, as the potion might give a temporary solution, but certainly no cure. No, the man would have to accept the fact that he is going bald and come to terms with the idea. Frankly, no-one notices you're going bald until you try to hide it. No - self-acceptance would be the key."

"So, there was no curse, then?"

"Of course not. Those women had no power to put a curse on him or anyone else, but they had the insight to play off people's insecurities – in this instance, that the man already had an appearance of a caricature of a pig. The lavender sold to them didn't have any power, either – they were clever at playing on people's hopes and fears." The vicar understood what I was telling him but didn't know how to resolve the problem.

"It's a shame we don't have a photo of the man so that we could see what other people see. More likely than not he has always had a bit of an upturned nose or what they call 'piggy-eyes' but we don't know that. Assuming he has one or other of these features, then he needs to accept the fact. If he doesn't, then the matter can still be resolved in the same way. First of all, he needs to be convinced that there is no curse on him. The women told him that the lavender they were selling would bring him good luck – but it hadn't brought them much good luck, had it? And they had bundles of the stuff. No, the man needs to understand they were charlatans, preying on the impressionable and weak-minded. They had not put any kind of a curse on him. If they put a curse on every person who refused to buy the lavender from them, I'd have to open a clinic.

"The man might have some pig features, but there the similarity ends. He is not 'becoming a pig' – he has no curly tail and no down-turned ears. He isn't covered in bristles and doesn't grunt or squeal. He doesn't wallow in mud and has good table manners. He isn't a glutton and doesn't stick his snout into a bucket of swill at the nearest opportunity. He is not, nor ever will be a 'pig'.

"The women were playing on his insecurities and had latched on to just the right thing to 'push his buttons' and get the response they wanted."

"So, what would you tell him to do?"

"Apart from all that silly curse malarky, he needs to concentrate on his other physical features. If he's tall – does he look like a giraffe? If he's short – does he look like a pygmy goat? If he's hairy – does he look like a gorilla? If he's skinny – does he look like a greyhound? He needs to recognise all his physical attributes and liken each one to an animal. If he does that, he will realise he is nothing like a pig. Have him look at himself each day and liken every part of him to another animal. He will come to realise he doesn't look like a pig at all and certainly isn't becoming a pig."

"I wish I had a tape-recorder so that I could write everything down you've told me," the vicar said.

I told the vicar he'd be fine, most importantly he had to convince the man he was not cursed – there was no curse.

I took my leave from the vicar and East London and went back to Maidstone. The Magister was recuperating at home. There was quite a backlog of work building up in the Sanctum and a few new potential clients. I rang the Magister – I would have called in to see him, but I still wasn't entirely sure where he actually lived. I knew it was somewhere off the Tonbridge Road, but I had no address.

He sounded perky enough and asked how my time in East London had gone. I told him all that had happened and then he surprised me. "I've had a call from Head Office," he said. "You have received a glowing report from the vicar you have been dealing with and it seems as though word is spreading of your abilities throughout the ecclesiastical community. I know this might not have been your chosen path, but we don't always get to choose which direction our work takes us. Do what you can in the Sanctum – my guess is you'll be off again soon. But don't worry about me – I'm on the mend, and I'll be back at work soon enough. Do what you need to do – there's nothing holding you here."

I sorted through the new enquiries we had received – some were simply resolved, others were complex or above my abilities, and then there were the daft ones. Before now, I hadn't realised how ridiculous some of the enquiries could be: 'I want you to help me find my cat'; 'I think there's a ghost in my grandad's greenhouse – all the plants are dying'; 'I want to win the Pools'; 'Can you put a curse on my neighbours? Their son keeps on kicking his football over the fence and it's squashed some of my hydrangeas' and so on.

I replied to them all courteously and professionally. There were a few follow-ons from work we'd done previously, but the questions I wasn't sure about I left for the Magister for when he would return.

I'd been back in Maidstone two or three days when I received another letter from Head Office. A church in East Sussex was experiencing some problems. Was I free to assist or at least to report back to Head Office? It would have been much more helpful if Head Office would be a bit more forthcoming about the nature of the enquiries to help me decide my suitability. I wrote back saying that I had some work to finish off in Maidstone and I also had to return to East London, but I would be free after that – if it was not too late.

I awaited their response and continued with my work. It was at this point that I received a letter from my friend Ignatius in Brighton. His letter was dark and lacking the joy I associated with him. The man known as 'Natalius' had been found dead in his bedsitting-room in Hove. He had taken a large quantity of the hallucinogen LSD and had subsequently hanged himself in his room. Ignatius supposed the paranoia and anxiety created by the constant misuse of the drug had overcome him. The police had found his naked, dangling body in a room filled with esoteric paraphernalia. Ignatius and the Magister were questioned by police. Ignatius knew nothing much about the man but believed he was heavily involved in some sort of cult. The Magister of Brighton kept his cards close to his chest and wouldn't speak to Ignatius about the incident. A death by misadventure was recorded.

Facilis descensus averno.

I wrote back and said I was sorry to hear about Natalius' suicide and hoped that his death didn't impact too heavily on their own lives and work. Perhaps I would try and visit when my current workload had subsided.

The Magister was re-admitted into hospital. I visited the Magister again and it was becoming apparent that his health was deteriorating. I didn't stay long – the man was in obvious need of sleep and I left him as he was drifting off. I asked the nursing staff to advise me of any changes and went back to my apartment.

The vicar in East London called me to say that he had managed to retrieve four of the effigies. The ceremonies I had suggested had worked wonders with his parishioners. The man I first questioned about the voodoo doll he had received had been diagnosed with a cataract and wanted to thank me for bringing this to his attention. I said I had a couple of errands to run and would be with him as soon as possible.

I returned to East London a couple of days later. The vicar gave me a very warm greeting and asked what it was I intended to do. He presented me with the four effigies. One of them appeared to be a bit singed – "Too near to the candle" he said, laughing.

I said I needed to get my haircut and would be back soon.

The hairdresser's shop (beg pardon, 'salon') was only a stone's throw away from the church, so I ambled my way down to it and watched the hairdresser at work through the window. He was a middle-aged man – about fortyish – who walked with a slight limp. Playing the 'Copy Cat Game' with this man would have been too easy. I made do with the haircut.

The hairdresser was a friendly man and was quite charming. Just as most hairdressers do, he asked about what holidays I had booked; what did I think of the football last Saturday and then we got on to matters of health. I told the man I was in fine health and told him I had noted that he walked with a slight limp.

"An old football injury," he said, and went on to tell me the whole story of how he came by his injury.

"Are you alright apart from that?" I asked, trying to glean as much information as I could while he trimmed around my ears.

"Well," he said, "we all get our aches and pains, I suppose. I'm not as young as I was. Get terrible calf cramps of a night, but we mustn't complain, must we?"

I said I pitied him having night cramps. I told him a friend of mine is kept up half the night with a pain in his buttocks and lower back. It was a lie of course but he wasn't to know that. It's amazing how such a small remark can have such terrible consequences – putting a suggestion such as this into the hairdresser's mind, thereby replicating the symptoms. I made a joke and said my friend was a right pain in the arse, which the hairdresser found funnier than my joke really was.

"Come back again, won't you?" he said as I left his salon.

I walked back to the church and told the vicar what I had learned. "Nice haircut, though!" the vicar said. I told him he was cheeky which brought a broad smile to his face.

"Right then," I said. "I need a little cardboard box."

"I've got just the thing," he said and emptied a little box of candles.

I told him the box would be perfect. "Now, pass me those effigies, can you, please?

I took out of my travel bag four little white pouches and put a doll into each one and laid them in the box. "You're not squeamish, are you?" I asked.

"Why?" the vicar asked as I pulled a dead rat out of my bag. The rat was wrapped in a plastic freezer bag. "What on Earth are you going to do with that?" he said, taking a step back from it.

"Just watch," I said, "it's magic!" and tied a noose around the rat's neck. I took a wooden skewer and inserted it almost full length into the lower spine of the rat and then a second into the animal's rectum. "There! That should do it!" I needed a fountain pen and paper which the vicar readily supplied. I wrote on it in large lettering 'Qui gladio vivit, gladio morietur' – 'he who lives by the sword shall die by the sword'. I wrapped up the rat in some black tissue paper which I had bought from W H Smith the day before, placed the rat and the written note into the box and sealed the box with sticky tape.

"Now we just need to deliver it," I said, which we did that night, leaving it in the shop's doorway.

"Is that it?" the vicar asked.

"That's plenty. The man will think he's targeted the wrong person and the strategically placed skewers will have just the psychosomatic response we're aiming for. "If you see a middle-aged man walking around here like he's got a bad dose of saddle rash, that'll most likely be him."

The vicar stifled a giggle. There was a look of sheer joy in his eye.

"If ever you come across a dead bird in the churchyard, drop it on his front step, would you, please? Let's keep him on his toes." The vicar agreed to do that.

I took my leave of the vicar and East London and got the train back to Maidstone. A note had been pushed through my letterbox asking me to call the hospital. It was late by the time I got home, so I rang them first thing in the morning.

Chapter 16

I called the hospital. The Magister was failing and the ward sister suggested I go and see him as soon as I was able.

"I need you to do something for me," the Magister said in a hushed voice. I told him I'd do anything for him. "I need you to make some tea."

"Tea?" I questioned him. "I don't think I can — not here. Perhaps one of the nurses?"

"No," he said emphatically, "you! I need you to make it. Here are the ingredients." He passed me a slip of paper. I knew all of the symbols written on it and I thought I knew what he was asking me to do. He saw the look of horror on my face. "Steady on," he said, "it's not that! Daft as a brush you are! As if!"

A nurse had looked over my shoulder and had seen the Magister's message. "You two speak Chinese? Oo I say, how interesting!" and took away the jug to fill with fresh water.

He squeezed my hand. "Trust me," he said. "Just trust me. Make the tea!"

I put the paper into my trouser pocket.

"You've been a good lad," he said. "An arsehole at times, but a good lad." He laughed and choked a little. "In my bag [which was on a chair at the side of his bed] is a letter addressed to me. Take it with you. Perhaps I should have let you see this years ago, but I never knew the right time." I took the letter from a zipped pocket on the front of his bag. "Don't read it now – when you get home. It might explain a few things for you. Now, off you go, you've got some tea to make." I took hold of his hand with both my hands and held it fast. I could feel tears beginning to form in the corners of my eyes. Looking deeply into my eyes as only he could, and gripping my hands firmly, he said "Go on, now - get yourself away. You've got some tea to make. There's nothing you can do here."

I let go of his hand and left his bedside and the ward, not looking back so he couldn't see the tears running down my cheeks. It wasn't until this moment had I come to realise how great the love and total respect was which I had for this little man.

My life was about to change forever and there was nothing I could do to stop it.

I don't think I need to tell you that this was the last time I saw the Magister.

I arrived home and sat down to read the letter.

'Flags, flax, fodder and frig!

Our blessings be upon you.

We, the followers of the Old Ones of the Wiccan Path, bestow great joy upon you. Take the gift we give you and mould and style it to make it quite your own.

Liberius is the name of your endowment. Take care of your charge for he is precious and is destined to lead not follow; to teach not learn; to bless not decry.

Liberius shall become known to you. You will know him by sight. Look for him and he will find you.

With the benediction showered upon you and the unction of the Old Ones, seek and safekeep your foundling.

Gerald of the Wiccan Order of the Druidic Path.

Flags for the stones wherein thee dwell,

Secured and fastened wish thee well.

Flax for the cloth thy back do bare,

Secured and fastened well thee fare.

Fodder for food you eat by day,

Secured and fastened on thy way.

Frig for the love from those and thee,

Secured and fastened ever be.

The wiccan wish be safe and sure,

Flags, Flax, Fodder and Frig for ever more.'

A lot of questions had been answered for me. Harry, my spirit guide, had shown me the letter but I had wrongly assumed it had been a letter to my mother, not to the Magister. However, another anomaly was now to be thrown into the mix – the letter was written when I was but four-years old – much as Harry had shown me and which my mother had confirmed.

I rather liked the Wiccan Blessing and memorised it. It could prove to be useful at some point.

I scrutinised the 'tea' recipe the Magister had given to me. My first thought was that it was some kind of palliative medicine. A more detailed examination threw up something I wasn't expecting.

To all intents and purposes this looked like a fairly simple but very strong sleeping draught. I had made something similar for a client some time ago, details about which I am unable to divulge – but this was much more potent. Then I realised that some elements of the potion were not wholly correct. Some inversions had been made, which almost looked like errors. I decided that the next day I would make the potion although this was no longer required – or so I thought at the time.

With the passing of the Magister (which was confirmed that evening) I couldn't help but wonder how things were going to 'pan out'. I called Head Office that evening but got no response, so I called again the following morning.

"Thank you for informing us," the administrator said. "There are protocols to follow in circumstances such as these. We will contact you directly. Please continue to work on as you are able." I said I would wait to hear further.

I didn't have to wait long. I received a return call within the hour. "I'm sorry to hear of your loss," the person (who failed to introduce herself) told me. "I'm sure you are aware that matters of this kind need to be dealt with, with care. Would you know if the Magister had family of any kind?"

I told them I didn't know of any – family was something the Magister never discussed. I knew nothing of his birth or background.

"I see you have been nominated as next of kin. It might be prudent to put an ad in the local paper (which was the Kent Messenger) telling of his passing and asking if there were any interested parties in his estate."

It was during this phone call I learnt that the Magister was ninety-one years old.

"Do you know if there is a will at all?"

I said I didn't know. The Magister never spoke of any personal matters.

"In situations such as these, regardless if there is a will or not, the Sanctum and the contents of his house return to the organisation. You can request any items, but any objects of a sensitive nature will not be given to you. Should any family members come forward, that will be dealt with by our administrators."

I told the caller that there was nothing I could think of that I might want. I had never seen inside the Magister's house – I wasn't even altogether certain where that was, so I could name nothing of any interest to me. There was only his Trilby, which I requested to keep for sentimental value.

"From our records, I see that the Sanctum is a rented premises. Is that correct?"

I said that as far as I knew, the Sanctum was rented from the home-owner of the property to which it was attached. I didn't know the home-owner's name or anything about the rental agreement.

"Don't worry – we have it all on record. We'll deal with that."

I asked what was to be done with the large collection of herbs and other ephemera in the Sanctum.

"I'll get back to you on that one. Meanwhile, it might be worth looking for an alternative premises. With the correct authority, these might be allowed to be transferred to a different Sanctum."

I said I would have a look around.

"No need to panic – these wheels turn very slowly." They would be in touch. They did ask if I could please confirm if I was still available to attend the appointment in East Sussex. There wasn't a lot I could do in Maidstone during this transition period, so I confirmed that I would still be able to take on the task.

"Good, I'll let them know. I'll send you the details in the post."

I knew they wouldn't put in writing what they wanted me to do - all they would send me would be contact details and an address. I said I'd await the letter.

"Sorry – before you go, I see there's a note on here. Sorry – give me a sec please, just putting you on hold a moment."

I said I'd wait.

"It looks like the Magisters have requested an interview with you – in person at Head Office. This was requested two weeks ago before your Magister died. I'll put these details into the letter with the other information. Is there anything else I can help you with?" The administrator sounded very much like a customer services agent. I said there was nothing else, thank you.

Just as I was about to put the receiver down, I caught the administrator asking for me again.

"Sorry," she said, "I nearly forgot. Do you drive?"

I said I didn't – I hadn't really had the need to learn.

"That's it," she said, "have a nice day!"

I thanked her. She must have been a customer service assistant in a former life.

The following morning, I went back to the Sanctum. I needed to get ready for my next assignment (whatever that happened to be) and I also wanted to look at the 'tea' recipe the Magister had given to me.

I studied what the Magister had written down. If all the symbols were inverted, this would have been a lethal concoction. But only two were inverted. I decided to make up the recipe as instructed.

We were getting low on some of the ingredients. How strange that I still chose to use the word 'we' here. The Magister's passing was going to take a while to adjust to. I made a note of stores that were needed. I had enough to make the potion, but was scraping the bottom of the barrel with some of the ingredients.

As I made the potion, it became obvious that this was not a sleeping draught at all. This was a hallucinogen, but a different one from those that I had used previously. My guess – and it was only a guess – was that this was a hallucinogen the Magister used for specific purposes – probably for use during evocations, but that was pure conjecture. He knew that he was dying and wanted to pass this on. Our time of learning had expired – I was on my own now, and had to find my own solutions. The Magister was helping me on my way beyond death.

I decanted the 'Magister's tea' into a plain glass phial. I named the Magister's tea 'Veneficus Scriptor Potum' and entered the recipe into my fourth Grimoire.

I had nothing to lose, so I packed the potion along with the other bits and pieces I thought I might need in East Sussex – the bell, a candle and stand, phials, pouches, alertness potions and the usual ephemera we used daily. I sorted through a few items of mail, took my bag and went home. I was now playing a waiting game – for details of my next assignment and communication from Head Office about what they intended to do with the Maidstone Chapter.

Chapter 17

The letter from Head Office arrived next morning. I was to travel to a town in East Sussex where I would be met at the train station. I was to call the MAD House after this assignment with reference to the interview they wished to conduct.

The letter didn't say much else, except to say they would be in touch further.

I took the bus – it was easier than going into and back out of London on a train. I waited at the train station entrance as I had been instructed to do for my pick-up. A taxi arrived and took me to my destination.

An old man in a dog-collar opened the front door of the vicarage, looked me up and down and said "You're young!" with not exactly a snarl, but a look of disapproval. This was going to be a very different liaison from the one in East London. I followed the old man into a conservatory at the back of the house.

He called out to the housekeeper - "Tea please, Agnes," and prompted me to sit in a wicker chair. Bits of wicker stuck into the back of my legs so I shuffled around a bit until I was comfortable.

"I didn't want you here at all," the vicar said. "It was the bishop insisted. I don't do with all your hocus-pocus mumbo-jumbo. Do you believe in God?" The man's manner was bordering on the hostile.

Agnes came in with the tea on a tray, and put it on a coffee table with a plate of biscuits. "I didn't say biscuits!" he barked at her. "He's come to work here – he's not a guest!"

Agnes said "Oh!" and leant across his shoulder to take the biscuits back again. As she did so, she looked straight at me and raised her eyes to heaven, with a little smirk rising from her lips.

"Well?" he said. "I asked you if you believe in God. Do you, or don't you? It's a simple question."

I told that him that at best I am non-committal.

"Non-committal!" he exclaimed. "That's the problem with your generation, you won't commit to anything! Non-committal!" he exclaimed again. This wasn't going to go well.

He asked me what my name was and I told him 'Liberius'. "You're named after a pope and you don't believe in God? That's outrageous! Blasphemous! You should be ashamed of yourself!"

I told him it wasn't my choice, but agreed it was a bit ironic.

"So," he went on, "tell me about yourself." I knew that telling him that I was unable to divulge this information would have rattled him all the more, so I abruptly changed the subject.

"I don't have much information about the problems your parish is experiencing." I told him. "Perhaps you could elucidate for me?"

The man leaned forward in his chair and sighed. "I wish I'd never told the bishop now," he said. "Mountains out of molehills – that's what this Is - mountains out of molehills."

I tried to be as professional as I could be and speak to him with as much courtesy as I could muster.

"I can appreciate your sentiments," I told him. "Something important to one person may seem a trifle to another. Perhaps we should humour your bishop? Would you be able to tell me what you told him? Maybe that would give me some idea about any potential problems you are experiencing?"

"Very well," he said, "if you put it like that. Before I start – the bishop's an idiot – I just thought you should know!" I raised a smile, took a sip of tea and got out my little notebook and pen and looked directly at the man to show I was intensely listening to him.

"You hit the nail on the head, young man. It's a trifle and probably nothing at all, but some of my parishioners have reported a problem."

I nodded and did as the Magister had taught me. I repeated what he said to show him I was paying close attention to what he was saying.

"Please can I ask what they have reported?"

"I am not only the vicar of this parish," he told me. "I am also Chaplain at two residential homes for the elderly. We used to call them 'old people's homes', but I got a slap on the wrist from the bishop last time I said that. That's where the problems are."

"You're a busy man," I said, buttering him up.

"Not really," he said. "I just sit around drinking tea, listening to people's problems. Some days I drink so much tea I think I should wear a tea cosy on my head. My bladder swells up like a barrage balloon!" He seemed to be warming to me a little. A very little.

"I enjoy your turn of phrase, Sir," I said, chuckling. Any amount of flattery would pay dividends in this situation.

"Hch hm," he cleared his throat. "I have my moments."

"So, are the problems being experienced in both care homes?" I asked.

"No – just the one. The other one's fine. Nothing reported there."

"Perhaps you could tell me what has been reported, if you'd be so kind."

"Yes, well, I'm not so sure about being kind, but I'll tell you anyway. It's only a small home - it has just eight residents. Two have advanced dementia which doesn't make it easy to sort the wheat from the chaff, so to speak. You have to take what they say with a pinch of salt."

I said I understood.

"But the other residents have reported some odd goings on – and the staff as well. We're struggling to keep staff there – they say they're... what was the word they used? Spooked. That's it, spooked."

"So, if I've understood you correctly – they say there are some unexplained things happening in the home? What kind of things – if you would, please?"

"Stuff being moved around, doors opening, things falling on the floor – that kind of thing."

"And just to reiterate – this is both the residents and the staff reporting these things?"

"Yes," he said, "both. If you ask me, it's just a load of old baloney. They seem to think there's a ghost or something."

"Please can I ask if anyone has seen any apparitions, or is it just the stuff moving about?"

"I don't think anyone has seen anything – or at least, if they have, they haven't told me."

"Have any of these incidents been documented? Written down or logged in any way?"

"Not so far as I know, but you could ask Matron – she'd be the best person to ask."

"Would it be acceptable for me to ask some of the residents and staff a few questions?"

"Knock your socks off," the man said. "Perhaps we could go there in the morning. I'll let Matron know we're coming. She's a hard cow but a good soul." I laughed again.

"What time would suit you, Sir?" I asked him.

"After breakfast. About ten?"

I said that would be perfect.

"Agnes will show you out – I need my afternoon kip." He called out for Agnes, who came into the room. "Show this young man out, will you Agnes, and point him in the direction of his B & B. See you tomorrow, *Liberius*." He spoke my name with some vehemence and a hint of a snarl.

I left the room and Agnes took me to the front door. "He's a funny old sod," Agnes said, "but you're lucky – you caught him in a good mood today."

"Thank heavens for that!" I said to the woman.

"Here," she said, passing me two Bourbon Creams wrapped up in a paper serviette. "Have these," she said. "Tight old bugger will never notice."

She pointed the way to the place I was to stay and I thanked her for the biscuits.

///

We left at ten the following morning as arranged. The Matron was a pleasant woman – stern, but friendly enough. The vicar introduced me as a 'friend'. I asked the Matron to tell me what had been going on with these strange incidents.

"It started about a month or so ago," she told me. "It started with little things – annoying things – misplaced hearing aids, things being in the wrong rooms, items of clothing going missing, residents' slippers being found outside – that kind of thing. Just silly but aggravating things. Then it started to get more peculiar. Cupboards being found open, residents complaining that family photographs were being turned upside-down, crucifixes being removed from walls and residents' teeth in other residents' rooms."

I asked when these instances occurred. Day or night – any particular time of day?

"Always during the day – we or the residents would find these strange things throughout the course of the day. Nothing ever happens in the night – we find things during the day – there's no specific time we find these things."

"Have you any thoughts about what might be going on here?" I asked her.

"Well, we've all talked about it, and a few of us – the staff – have suggested someone playing silly buggers, and others –

one in particular – thinks we've got a ghost. I mean, a lot of residents have died here, but I think that's a bit far-fetched."

"Would you have a record of when these things occurred, please? Is there a pattern involved?"

"I've looked into it in case it is someone just making mischief, but I can't find one," she told me.

"Would it be acceptable for me to question some of the staff, please?"

"I don't see why not. We're a small team here. We have six permanent staff members and a couple of bank staff who cover holidays – that kind of thing."

I asked who was rota'd on for today.

"Just three," she told me. "and the cook and her assistant, oh, and there's a cleaner. They've all been here for years. They're all quite upset about it."

"Is there somewhere I could use to speak to them, please?"

"Yes, you can use my office - I've got my rounds to do. Do you think you'll be long?"

"I can't imagine so," I told her.

"Good. I'll go and get one of them. Are you coming with me, Reverend, or are you staying here?"

"I'll hang on here, thank you," the vicar said. "I want to see what this monkey's up to," nodding in my direction.

The matron raised an eyebrow, but left the room saying nothing more.

"What do you think?" the vicar asked when the Matron was gone. "Do you think it's someone just messing about? Do you believe in ghosts? I don't know what you believe in, Mr Non-Committal."

"Let's see what the staff have to say," I suggested. "I don't want to make any preconceived judgements."

"You should have been a politician – you never answer a question outright."

I chuckled. "Ghosts are just apparitions," I told him. "Like recordings in time, usually associated with nearby running water. Don't ask me why – I don't think anyone knows why. They can't interact with the living or cause harm. They simply appear and then disappear – a faint recording of a past event."

"Well, that's as clear as mud. Thank you for that." The vicar sat disgruntled in his armchair.

One by one, the Matron brought the three carers in to speak to me. They told me about what they had witnessed and one in particular seemed genuinely frightened.

And then I questioned the cleaner. "I can communicate with the dead," she told me. "I tell you now, it's a ghost doing it and 'is name is Jack."

The cleaner was an unusual woman. She told me that she was a spiritualist who "'ad a gift like me mother 'ad. I tell ya now, it's Jack. I tried to tell the uvvers, but they don't listen none.

Fink I'm daft. Fink I'm a bit potty. I *know* what I'm talking about. It's obvious, ain't it? All these things what's goin' on. It's not me what's a bit potty – it's them!"

I thanked her for her very useful information and she left to go about her business.

"It's her, isn't it?" the vicar said.

"I think so," I said, agreeing with him.

We agreed that she was doing these things to try to prove to the rest of the staff that she had a 'gift' and that she could communicate with the dead.

"How do we solve it?" the vicar asked. "We can't accuse her, can we? *Can* we?"

I said I needed some time to make sure we were right in our conclusion and that an answer would be forthcoming. I really did need the time – not to find a solution – that was easy enough – but to make sure that this was the problem and nothing else was going on that I needed to know about.

"Thank you for helping with this," I said to the Matron when she came back to her office.

"You're very welcome," she replied. "I hope you can get to the bottom of it."

"I hope so," I said. "You've been so helpful so far, I wonder if I can put on you again?"

"What do you want?" she asked. She could sound quite abrupt, but I think that was due to spending years in her profession. Sometimes you have to be hard to get the results you are after.

"I need a room to work in," I said.

"Isn't this one good enough? What's wrong with it?"

"I'm sorry, I need a room without distractions such as clocks or ornaments – I need to concentrate. Perhaps just a little room with just a table and a chair? Would you have a room like that?"

"Not really," she said. "There's a cupboard on the first floor. It's got a few bits and pieces in it – I suppose we could take them out?"

"It sounds ideal," I said.

"What do you want it for?" the vicar interjected.

"Meditation," I said.

He pulled a face like he had just detected a foul smell.

"Come on then," the Matron said and led the vicar and me to the cupboard. There wasn't much in there - a mop and a bucket, a large pack of toilet rolls and a broken chair.

"That's perfect!" I said.

"Glad you think so!" the Matron replied. "You get that stuff out and I'll find you a table.

She went into the room next door and I heard her say "Just borrowing your table, Doris. Be back in a minute," and she trundled the table on casters out into the corridor.

I said I needed to concentrate and could not be disturbed. "OK," the Matron said. "I'll put a notice on the door if you like – 'Danger - do not enter' and I can lock it. I'll give you a key to get out though, when you've finished 'meditating'," making the sign for inverted commas. "Just stick this stuff in the corridor – there shouldn't be a need for anyone to go in there. If there's a fire in the meantime, I can blame you for blocking the fire escape."

I overheard the matron and the vicar talking as they left me in the corridor.

"Who the hell is he?"

"The bishop sent him."

"Oh!"

I hadn't tried to contact Harry on my own before. This was a new experience for me and one I was unsure about. I knew how to summon him, but I couldn't ring the bell myself, so I was uncertain how to ground myself. I had nothing to lose, so I went ahead with the evocation.

I took a small sip of the new potion the Magister had jotted down for me – forever known as the 'Magister's Tea'. I didn't speak out loud, but thought the words I needed in my head.

The colours and shapes were brighter than before and I could sense Harry's presence already. A plethora of images came into vision, none of which I had previously seen and none made any sense to me. Drinking the Magister's tea had very different results from other potions I had used. I could hear

Doris in the room next door calling to the carer "They've got my table!" so that was grounding enough.

I put the question to Harry about the goings-on at the home. He led me into the beautiful garden I had been in before and took me along the path and into the shed. Some papers were laid on the table. Next to the papers were the mop and bucket I had just put into the corridor. I thanked Harry for confirming my suspicions – he was indicating by showing me these items that the cleaner was the perpetrator of the unusual activity in the home. I wanted to know if anything was afoot in the building – such as a spirit, and questioned Harry accordingly. I was led out of the shed and through the garden to a pond and a fountain. I was beckoned to drink. I took another sip of the 'tea'.

Doris's voice still rang out in the corridor. The second sip of the Magister's tea gave me a far more lucid vision.

From the fountain, I was taken to the outside of the building I was in. I could see residents in their bedroom windows, but instead of faces they had flowers for heads. I did not venture inside. Instead, I was taken to a walled garden. All the plants were dead inside it. Nothing was alive. Graves marked the names of the flowers.

Doris's voice called out again and I came out of my trance.

There was nothing else prevalent in this home. The dead remained dead. No other spirits were at play here, much to my relief.

I wheeled the table back into Doris's room, said 'thank you' and returned the mop and bucket and other things into the cupboard and locked the door.

I found the vicar asleep in an armchair in the resident's lounge, his mouth wide open, snoring loudly. I gave him a gentle nudge on his shoulder.

"By God, you take your time," he said.

I apologised and said we needed to speak to the cleaner again. He agreed, so we went off to speak to the Matron. We came across the cleaner on our way and we three sat down on some seats in a corridor. I did the talking under the distrustful watch of the vicar.

"I just wanted a quick word with you, if that's OK?" I said to her, to which she assented. "I want to thank you for talking to us earlier - I am really very grateful. I also want to thank you for the most valuable information you have given us. It has made a tremendous difference. I think I'm right in saying that we couldn't have done this without you."

I nodded to the vicar who agreed. "I think you have a God-given gift," I continued. "You have a great insight into these things, and I want to thank you for sharing this with us."

The woman had a smug grin on her face. I continued: "I want you to do something for me, if you feel you are able to do it." The woman nodded eagerly. She had got the recognition she had so craved. "You can talk to Jack, can't you?" I asked her. She said that yes, he talked to her all the time. "I need you to ask him to stop what he is doing. I think it is only you who is able to do this. Of course, if you don't believe your gift is strong enough, then please tell me now."

"Oh no, I can do that," she said, "quite gladly, Mister!"

"Perhaps," I said, "we could thank Jack for his help in this matter. Are you able to tell me if Jack was a former resident here?" She said he was. I went on – "I couldn't help but notice on my way in that there is a bare spot in one of the rose beds right in the middle of the lawn. Have you seen it?"

The woman said she hadn't noticed it. "I think it would do Jack a great service if something was planted there in his memory. You see, it seems to me that Jack feels forgotten and it's only by doing all these annoying things does he get the attention he so much desires. Perhaps a nice little rose bush and a name plaque underneath it. It doesn't need to be anything elaborate or expensive – just a simple plaque stating his name and maybe something about yourself. How about 'In loving memory of Jack with much love – and then your name', in recognition of what you have achieved. How would you feel about that?"

"I think it's lovely. That poor man – fancy being forgotten like that. I'll happily do it. What colour rose do you think?"

"I think Jack will direct you. He'll show you."

"Thank you – I think you've done a wonderful thing. Gawd bless you."

As we left the building on the way back to the car, the vicar said two simple words – "Clever bastard!"

155

Chapter 18

The vicar invited me to dinner that night in the rectory. "Agnes does a lovely roast," he said, and I told him I would be honoured to join him.

"I apologise," he said as we started to eat. "I was a bit harsh with you yesterday. I can be a silly old fool sometimes. I judged you without knowing you, and for that I am very sorry."

I told him there was no need for an apology. I had enjoyed working with him and thought we made a good team."

"Mmm... don't push it!" he said and laughed.

We talked for a good couple of hours. He was really quite congenial given the right circumstances and several glasses of sherry.

"It's a shame you can't tell me more about yourself," he said, "but I understand your need for privacy. It just makes the whole caboodle look more 'cloak and dagger' than it actually is – to my mind, unnecessarily so."

"There's honestly not an awful lot to know," I told him. "I come from a very ordinary world. I was taken under someone's wings, trained, educated and then released into the community to do what I was taught to do. It wouldn't have been much different if I had taken on an apprenticeship as a tradesman and then come to fix your windows."

"You've never thought of taking up the cloth, I suppose?" I told him he was the second person to ask me that. "You've just got the right way about you – you've that way of speaking and connecting with people."

I thanked him for the compliment.

"I want to ask you something," he said. "By all means tell me no, but I'd be interested to know. It's to do with this!" He pointed to his leg. "I get the gout something awful. It's not too bad at the moment, but it makes me terrible crotchety when it flares up. Is there anything you can recommend for it? I'm sure you have access to herbs and all that malarky – I was just wondering."

I told him I could help, but he might not like the answer.

"Hit me with it," he said, "as long as you don't have to go into a little room all on your own again."

I laughed. "No," I said, "and don't worry – it's not the dreaded hocus-pocus mumbo-jumbo, either. The cure is simpler than you might imagine."

"Go on," he said, "I'm all ears."

"Every morning, take a clean glass and fill it will spring water – anything out of the supermarket will do. It doesn't matter if it's still or sparkling, but it must be fresh spring water. Put the glass of water under your bed. Make sure you change the glass and water each morning. Don't reuse the glass or reuse the water. It must be fresh water in a clean glass each day."

"Are you pulling my leg?"

I told him I wasn't joking. "I wouldn't dream of pulling your leg – not with that gout!" He raised a smile and nodded, enjoying my flippancy. I said "Try it. You might be surprised."

"Mmm… I'll think about it." Whether or not the vicar took my advice I never found out. It would have been interesting to know – this was one cure which I knew had worked previously.

[If any reader of my memoirs suffers from gout or night cramps – give this a try. You have nothing to lose and maybe a peaceful night to gain!]

///

I left the vicar and the next day I returned to Maidstone. I was greeted by a letter from Head Office on my doormat.

I was requested to attend a formal interview on the 9th of the following month at Head Office. They added a post script to the bottom of the letter. "This is not a disciplinary interview. Your compliance will be appreciated."

I had three days, so I had time to put some matters in order in the Sanctum. Post was building up, so I replied to the most urgent, apologising for the delay in my response. The Sanctum had started to smell musty – it smelled of decaying organic matter, which I felt I should mention at my interview. If no novitiate was forthcoming, whatever they were thinking of doing with the Maidstone Chapter, I needed help.

I did what I could in the Sanctum over the next couple of days and journeyed up to Head Office.

Head Office was a rambling old building with an overgrown garden and the need of a good lick of paint. If you didn't know, you would think it was a disused farm house.

I was ushered into an austere waiting room and offered a cup of tea which I accepted.

"You can bring the tea in with you," a man standing in a doorway told me.

He led me into another grimly decorated room. A single chair sat in the middle of the floor in front of three elderly gentlemen who were sat behind a long table, which was clothed to the floor. Only the man in the middle of the three spoke.

"Welcome!" he announced. "We have been waiting to see you. I trust we find you well?" He was quietly cheerful. I said I was very well, thank you.

He thanked me for attending the interview. I said I was pleased to come and interested to see Head Office.

"Yes," he said. "I'm afraid we're not quite what we were. Back in the day, this was the place to be."

I said the place was old but had a lot of charm.

"Yes," he answered, "we've heard you're a born diplomat," and he smiled broadly. "Don't look so nervous, you're not here for a telling off – quite the opposite, in fact."

His reassurances did little to help calm me.

"We've been getting some extraordinary reports about you. You seem to be making friends in quite high places. Before we get on with the interview, I need to inform you about your current circumstances and that of the Maidstone Chapter. We are very sorry to hear of the loss of your Magister. He was a great man and will be sorely missed. There are some protocols we need to inaugurate – I'm sorry if these seem a little harsh to you."

I said it was alright and that I understood there were rules in place which were intended to make these things easier, however distasteful they might be.

"Firstly, don't worry about organising the funeral or having anything to do with the funeral arrangements. All such matters will be carefully managed. The Magister's house will be cleared and all documentation relative to the organisation will be archived. The Magister had not made a will and we have not been able to trace any living relatives. After careful sorting through the Magister's effects, you will be offered any of his possessions prior to the rest of his belongings being collected by a house clearance company. All objects stored in the Sanctum are the property of the organisation to do with as seen fit. Are you OK with all of that?"

I said it was fine.

"As nominated next of kin, all monetary savings the Magister may have possessed will be bequeathed to you, regardless as to whether any further family can be traced. This will include any gains made from the auction of his belongings - after any outstanding debts have been paid, naturally. Nothing can be removed from the Sanctum without the express permission of the organisation."

I nodded my understanding.

"Good. We request that you sign this document agreeing to what has just been disclosed to you."

The document and a pen were passed to me and I signed it.

"With regards to the Maidstone Chapter, we have decided that a new Magister will be assigned to it. We do not feel that this would be the right time to give you accession to the title. I'm sorry if this news is a disappointment to you. It's not that we do not feel you are ready or unable to take the reins as it were, but we have a different path we would like you to consider taking. We do ask though that you assist the new Magister to become familiar with his new calling, and we suggest a period of sixth months for this transition. Are you happy to be compliant with this request?"

I said I was, but secretly I was disappointed that I was not offered the position. I supposed my time would come.

"With regards to your own career path, we are in one accord that you be offered a new tenure. In light of your recent successes, you will be designated Magister Legatus Sine Officio. In effect, this makes you a roving ambassador for the organisation, but without defined office. For the immediate future, your work will be closely aligned to ecclesiastical enquiries. In accepting this position, after the sixth-month transition period of the Maidstone Chapter, you would be working where you are requested to work at any given time.

As Magister Legatus, you would be free to accept or decline any line of work requested of you. If you feel that any work is above your level of ability or outside of your remit, we ask you to acknowledge this in writing, with the reasons for your rejection of the request. Is all this clear to you so far?"

I said I believed I understood what they were suggesting for me.

"In light of this tenure, should you wish to accept it, it would be of great help to provide your own transport. To this end, the organisation will help you to attain a driving licence and if successfully completed, you will be designated a company car to assist you in the execution of your duties. Although employed as a roving ambassador, we advise keeping your current lodging as a base from which you can travel where and when necessary. Do you have any family commitments?"

I said I had none.

"That is as it should be. We apologise for the formality of these proceedings, but we wish to be as clear as possible as to what your duties will be and the method of implementation. Do you have any questions for us before we continue?"

I asked if I was able to take my grimoires from the Sanctum.

"Yes. These form part of your work and as such can be considered a crucial component of your role. Do you have any further questions for us at this point?"

I said I didn't. My new role intrigued me.

"Good. Please can we ask what training, if any, you have in religious teaching?"

I had only been to Sunday School at the Assembly of God Church in Brewer Street as a child, under duress. Mum would dress me up smartly and I would go kicking and screaming, preferring to go out on my bike with my friends. I remembered stories like Daniel in the Lion's Den and the Battle of Jericho, but other than that, my education was severely limited. Being cast as 'Rabbit Number 3' in the school nativity play seemed not worthy of mention.

"We thought that might be the case. Please can we ask who your guiding spirit or spirits are currently?"

I told them my spirit guide was called Harry.

"Thank you." The three gentlemen whispered to each other.

"There is a spirit guide who specialises in all church matters. We think that contact with this spirit will be beneficial to you. The spirit calls itself Eusebius. Eusebius can be difficult to connect with, but Harry should be able to introduce you to him. We will assist you in this and contact can be made before leaving us today. Magister Cornelius will support you." He motioned towards the man sitting to his left.

I thanked them for this information and confirmed that I would ask Harry for his assistance.

"We have received a plethora of enquiries from ecclesiastical quarters, which is part of the reason for considering you as the roving ambassador to the church. In this capacity, you will report directly to us at Head Office. Any supplies you need

163

after the sixth month transition period can be acquired directly from Head Office *'sine explicatione'* [without question]. Is that understood?"

I said it was clear. We finished the meeting and Magister Cornelius took me to a side room, where I successfully (with the assistance of Harry) made contact with Eusebius. Eusebius was very well educated and I got the distinct impression he would have preferred to speak to someone with a bit more of a background in religious matters.

All documentation was signed and sealed, and the Magister pulled me to one side to have a coffee with him.

"Just off the record," he said, "we are experiencing difficulty recruiting novitiates at the moment. Not so much recruiting, but *retaining* novitiates. Can I ask your opinion, using your own history, what the problem might be?"

I told him that Latin was a big hurdle to overcome. He agreed that Latin had always been an obstacle yet a necessity. "It not only gives us the unambiguity we need, but also gives us an air of mystery which serves us so well."

I said I understood, but it was a pity that the study of Latin was such a deterent.

"What else might be the problem?" he asked.

"No pointy hats," I told him. "Reality does not reflect expectation. Common literature, and in particular film and television, give a false impression of our profession. It could be quite disappointing to a newcomer. There's also the increasing distance put between us and our relatives and friends. That might well put a lot of people off from continuing." I also told him about the two novitiates who left when confronted with spiritualia.

"But you didn't experience these hindrances yourself?"

I said I definitely did, but I persevered with my studies and got over my misconceptions and prejudices.

"Is there one thing that you would say encouraged you to persist, when others might fail?"

"The Magister." He nodded his understanding.

I returned to Maidstone to prepare for my new vocation as Magister Legatus Liberius.

Magister Legatus

Chapter 19

As a race of people, we dislike change. Just as Maidstone had changed beyond recognition since my childhood, I was not the same person, either. Life moves on and we cannot hold back the surge of change in our lives.

Magister Victor joined me in the Maidstone Chapter. A little older than me, he was affable enough, but was very different and worked contrarily to the old Magister.

I gave him a tour of Maidstone and showed him the highlights and lowlights of the town. He had come from a much smaller Chapter, and the size of Maidstone made him feel that he had ventured into a vast metropolis. Perhaps he wasn't wrong.

We cleaned out the decaying herbs and other ephemera and replaced them whence we were able. A small unit had become available in a small industrial estate, and I put forward an application to Head Office to relocate the Sanctum.

I passed my driving test on my second attempt. I would have passed on my first, but thick fog and a reversing milk float put paid to that.

A note had been pushed through my letterbox from my mother informing me that my brother was now married and had two children. Perhaps I should pay a visit to him and his family, but family tethers were now so dissolved I didn't quite see the point in going to see him. It was a shame I couldn't relate to my mother my success in my chosen profession.

As promised, my first commission as Magister Legatus was received after the six months' transition period. I was requested to go to a diocese in the West Country. As usual, I was given no details of the task in hand. Victor suggested they didn't like to put things in writing, which was a valid point and made sense. It was still annoying, though.

My company car had yet to materialise, so I took the lengthy train journey to my destination. This was to be my first foray into the Roman Catholic Church – which was even more of a mystery to me than the Protestant one.

The case revolved around a priest who had contacted the organisation. He had developed a close attachment to a female parishioner. The relationship, he claimed, was purely platonic. The woman was a widow and they had struck up the friendship simply by association. Both he and the woman were lonely. The priest was in his early fifties and had spent the majority of his life alone. He enjoyed the friendship the two had struck up and had no intention of ending their liaisons.

The problem was this – he and the woman involved had been receiving some troubling messages by post. One such message had been stapled to an oak tree in the churchyard. They were being accused of all kinds of improprieties. The priest had informed the police, but as the messages contained nothing in the form of a threat, they were unable to assist.

Push had come to shove when the same mystery accuser had written to the bishop, telling him of the immodesties committed by the priest and the woman. The priest was in danger of being defrocked and it was at this point that the priest had contacted the MAD House.

"Before we proceed further," I informed him, "I need your assurance that there is no truth to these accusations."

He assured me there were none, but in his heart of hearts, had his life taken a different path, then there would have been a serious possibility that the relationship could have progressed in a different direction.

"Do you have any idea at all who could be behind these allegations?"

"None whatsoever," he told me. "If we could find out who is behind these terrible rumours, perhaps we could draw them to a close?"

I said it was a possibility but not guaranteed. People who take a holier-than-thou approach tend to be difficult to dissuade in their beliefs.

We spent the first day reviewing the messages which had been received – nothing written in them suggested the possible source. The priest was a genial fellow and had been deeply hurt by these accusations of misconduct. I said I would sleep on it.

What I really needed was to question Harry – he may be able to point me in the right direction. I couldn't see at this point that Eusebius would be much help in this situation. Next day, I made contact with Harry before going to see the troubled priest.

Harry, as is his wont, led me into the beautiful garden and on to the shed in the corner. We did not go inside the shed, but he showed me a patch of garden which had been taken over by bind weed. A tangled mass was suffocating everything in its path. The image changed and the patch of contaminated garden was transported to the front of an ordinary looking house. Bind weed was creeping through the door and the windows. A woman was watering and feeding the bind weed to make it grow stronger, when it should have been destroyed, not pampered.

From what Harry had shown me, it would seem that the female friend of the priest was the source of the problem. She was making things worse, fuelling the problem but for what purpose?

I questioned Harry for a second time. Again, I was led into the garden. At first, it looked like it was snowing and then then snow turned into petals. Masses of petals fell all around. These were not just petals – this was confetti. My view changed suddenly. This was unusual for Harry – images usually changed gradually. Eusebius had joined us. I was inside a church, looking towards the altar. Into view came an image of the priest, completely naked, 'defrocked', with bind weed crawling up his body. I had some terrible news to give to the priest.

I needed the priest to work out what was happening for himself. I could not be the harbinger of such upsetting findings.

"Tell me," I asked, "could you tell me how you have come to know your friend?" I did call the woman by name, but I am unable to do so here.

"Well, it's pretty straightforward," he said. "She and her husband were members of the congregation. As such, I came to know them quite well. They were regular members – they came to Mass weekly. You get to know your frequent worshippers."

I said I expected that was the case. "And when did she lose her husband?"

"It would have been about three years ago. Cancer – such a shame – he was a good man and a good husband."

"Did they have children?"

"A son – he's in the army – deployed in Bosnia."

"So, your friend is very much alone – when her son's away, that is."

"Very much so. I think she feels abandoned – by both her son and her husband."

"That's very sad. Does she have a close circle of friends?"

"Some – but not close. She has always been a family-based person. She does have friends, but they have families of their own. I'm her best friend, I suppose."

"That must be a great consolation to her – to have such a good friend. Tell me, you said to me earlier that things could have been very different if it wasn't for your priesthood. Has she confessed the same thing to you?"

"Confessed? I think you mean 'admitted'." My choice of words embarrassed me. Something to consider in the future.

"Apologies, yes, admitted. Has she told you much the same thing?"

"Not in so many words. She describes us as the 'odd couple'."

"I'm sorry to say this, but you used the word 'couple' there. There are many meanings to the word, so I apologise if I say this indiscreetly – do you think, in any way, she sees you as a 'couple' – not as two friends or as just two people?"

"Mmm… interesting question. I hadn't quite thought about it like that. Perhaps – but I don't think so."

"If she does see you as a couple, as said in common parlance, are there any situations or circumstances which might confirm this to her?"

"Well, no. She's never said as much."

I sat and thought without speaking. "You know my calling," I said, "and you know that we do things in different ways – you and me. We each use esoteric means to achieve an end result. You use prayer, whereas I do things a little differently. As much as your means are a mystery to me, mine will be a mystery to you. Am I right in saying that?"

"Yes, quite. I don't know quite what it is you do."

"Essentially, I try to put order into chaos. Sometimes, we need clarity where there is none. Please can I suggest we use a simple but different method to achieve this? There's no hocus-pocus, nothing which you might call 'occult' – I simply suggest a way to see things with greater clarity than we do now."

He assented, reluctantly.

I took a phial out of my bag. "What's that?" he said with his eyes wide open, looking like I was about to poison him.

"Nothing that could cause any harm," I told him. "It might not taste very nice, but you only need a drop, trust me."

"Trust me, he says! Well, we'll see."

The phial contained water and sour flavouring only. I asked the priest to take a sip of the potion (which I called an elixir in this case). He grimaced with the tartness of the liquid. "Good God, man!" he said, "Are you trying to kill me?"

I laughed and said "Close your eyes, please." I then recited the words 'Da nobis facultatem videndi et virtutem intelligendi et virtutem reparandi quod fractum est' [Give us the ability to see and the strength to understand and the power to repair that which is broken]. I hoped he might be able, at some level, to understand the words spoken, or at least in part. If he didn't, it was of no matter.

He looked up at me as I spoke the words. "Eyes closed, please," I said. "We need to concentrate." He did as I bid.

I talked him through some basic questions and asked him to answer as truthfully as he was able.

"Can you suggest any reason why someone would be trying to sully your image?"

"No."

"Have you knowingly upset anybody recently?"

"There was a family of a suicide – I wouldn't allow the deceased to be buried on consecrated ground, but as far as I know, they came to accept the decision. I can't think of anyone else."

"How do you feel about your female friend? Be as honest as you can."

"I admire her greatly, but I'm not in love with her. I think I'm beyond that."

"And how do you think she feels about you?"

"I'm not sure. She knows the situation we're in and that it isn't possible to change that."

"If she really wanted to alter the situation, how might she be able to achieve that?"

"Well, apart from getting me defrocked, or me resigning, there's nothing could be done."

He looked up at me, frowning. "Are you trying to suggest..."

"I suggest nothing. You are applying a suggestion."

"She wouldn't, would she? Surely, she wouldn't try to get me defrocked so that we could marry? Surely not! I mean, why send me such lurid letters."

"I don't know all the answers, I'm afraid. Perhaps she is trying to instigate a thought in your head – a subtle suggestion or a spark of what could be?"

"Oh my God! How did I not see?"

"Sometimes, when we're in a situation we have to look at it from a different perspective. As they say, you can't see the wood for the trees."

"Well, bless my soul! Who'd've thought? What should I do?"

"As far as I can see, you have a choice to make – let her down gently, or do the unthinkable and resign. Not a very nice choice, but the choice is yours."

"Mmm.." he mused. "Be Narziss and not Goldmund."

I was glad I knew to what the priest was referring. I had managed (after several attempts) to finish reading Herman Hesse's novel. For those who are unaware of the book, this is story of two friends who grow up in a monasterial school. Narziss stays on at the monastery, whereas Goldmund leads a debauched life in the real world. The gist of the tale is the difference between a spiritual or more worldly existence and the quest for the meaning of life.

"Quite," I said in agreement. "I can't choose for you. You have to find your own path."

The priest thanked me.

A phone call came through to me from Head Office. I was asked to leave the West Country and journey to Manchester for another assignment.

Chapter 20

After dealing with two warring vicars in Manchester, a lack of promotion in Coventry, a haunting in Ripon, a church thief in Lowestoft, and half a dozen or so other ecclesiastical assignments, I finally made it back home to Maidstone. A clapped-out Ford Escort was parked outside my rooms in Peel Street and the keys to it had been pushed through my letterbox. I thought they really could have found me something better, but truth be told, it saw me through from 1992 through to the year 2002 with few problems. The years were rolling on and I barely noticed them pass by.

I was in serious need of a new wardrobe. Washing out shirts and underwear in hotel sinks had taken its toll, and I realised I was looking not only older than I'd liked to be, but I was beginning to have the appearance of being scruffy. I looked in the mirror and saw Worzel Gummidge looking back at me. A shopping trip in my newly acquired car was just the ticket.

The street system in Maidstone had changed beyond all recognition - the army barracks on the Sandling Road had been demolished; the main thoroughfare through Maidstone – Chatham Road - was now a back street renamed 'Old Chatham Road'; the allotments near to the Sanctum had gone and a tangle of a one-way system wound its way around Maidstone like a reticulating python, squeezing the life out of anything it

176

its path. I found my way back home without stopping the car. I'd try another day. Perhaps I'd walk instead.

I called Head Office and there was nothing pressing, so they suggested taking a week's holiday. I called Ignatius and spent a pleasant week in Brighton, discussing all that was happening to us, what we'd done and the mistakes we'd made. The sea breeze and the conversation were refreshing.

Ignatius had been given a new project – recruitment. As I was now, he was to become a roving Magister, visiting the numerous Chapters, ascertaining needs – in particular, the needs of the novitiates to try to retain their fealty. He seemed to be the ideal candidate for the task – he had a good way with people, in particular young people, so his vocation was apt for him. "Look at the two of us," he said, "both Magisters with not a pot to piss in." He was right of course. Neither of us had anything much to call our own – not even a workplace, but in our own ways it didn't matter. We were quite content and enjoying our new challenges.

I returned home after a week away and awaited instruction. Victor had a new novitiate and there wasn't room for all three of us in the small Sanctum, so I returned to my rooms. Renting the unit on the industrial estate had fallen through, but a new unit out at Lenham looked promising. It was only a Portacabin in the corner of a builder's yard, but it was undisturbed and all but invisible from anywhere except inside the yard.

I was recalled to Head Office. There was either going to be a change to my line of work or something else was afoot. They had a bad habit of not giving the game away as to their intentions. It was nice to able to drive there rather than taking two trains and a bus. King of the Road!

I arrived at the MAD House. The reason for speaking to me in person was due to the sensitivity of the case which I needed to be aware of in depth.

A bishop was retiring – but that statement isn't entirely true. A bishop's mental health was failing and it had been suggested that he should retire. He had unwittingly been making some rather distressing mistakes – one of which was at a funeral when he thought he was giving a wedding speech. He couldn't be forced to retire, but it was strongly suggested that he do so, which he did under duress. He didn't fully comprehend why his retirement was necessary.

There were two nominees for the position. I had been asked to suggest the suitability of either candidate. The bishop was not in a correct state of mind to suggest a successor. It wasn't until much later that I find out the high station of the requester.

I had been given the authority to question both nominees and anyone else I considered worthy of interview, but I was not to question the retiring bishop, whose testimony would be in doubt. Neither candidate was to know the identity of the other and neither was to know that they had been nominated. If neither was deemed to be suitable, then that should form the basis of my report. There had been some problems retaining staff in the bishopric, and an insight into the state of affairs was also requested.

In my naïvete, I thought this would be a simple matter, but soon found out this was not so much about who was most suited to the role, but who might create the lesser nuisance if elected. Another well thought-of bishop had been in some controversy of late, which had generated some bad press coverage. A repetition of this error would be most unwelcome and a further blight on the Church.

To make this narrative more comprehensively understood, I have named the two candidates considered for the bishop's office Candidate A and Candidate B. Other interviewees I call Interviewee C, D and E. I am quite sure that you understand I can neither tell you their names nor the bishopric concerned.

I drove to the city, found lodgings close to the cathedral, checked in and left my briefcase there. The Canon Chancellor greeted me on the Cathedral steps. He had been informed that he was to expect a 'Special Envoy'. He had been instructed to give me access to any information I requested. I was given a new name for this special assignment – Father Nicholas. I was under instruction not to divulge the purpose of my visit. I was used to this type of secrecy so was not fazed by it.

"Welcome!" he said, shaking my hand. "Come in, come in!" He led me into his office.

I said I was sorry to hear that the bishop was in ill-health. "Yes," he said, "it's very sad. Lovely man. I suppose you heard about the funeral debacle?"

I said I had heard something about it but was unaware of the details.

"Terrible! Terrible thing to happen. A sister from the Convent attached to the cathedral had passed away. The funeral, thanks be to God, was held privately in the Convent. The bishop became confused and told some very ribald jokes, believing himself to be conducting a wedding speech. Even for a wedding speech, the jokes were far from acceptable. A priest who was *in situ* managed to get the bishop off the platform, but it caused a terrible commotion. The Sisters were very upset."

I told him I could understand the consternation the episode had caused them. "And how is the bishop now?"

"Deteriorating. I shouldn't wonder if he'll retire soon."

I said I could understand that. "I was wondering if you could show me around your cathedral?" I asked, changing the subject. "I haven't been before - it looks magnificent!"

The Chancellor showed me the cathedral with glee. The history, the vaults, the treasury – it was a beautiful edifice.

"I've been asked to provide you with whatever you need," he said, "but to be honest, I've no idea what that might be."

I said I'd let him know. "Perhaps you might find me a list of the priests and clerical staff associated with this bishopric – if it's not too much trouble."

"No trouble at all. Would tomorrow be acceptable?"

"More than acceptable," I said.

"Excuse me for asking," he said, "but I notice you're not wearing any kind of clerical clothing."

"I'm not on an ecclesiastical mission," I said. "Best to be incognito." He said he understood, but I could see by the look on his face he was not convinced. We agreed to meet up the following morning. "Will it be alright to have a look about on my own for a while? I want to get a feel for the place."

"No problem at all. We lock the main door at half five, but if you need more time, please just ask."

I thanked him for his kind assistance and went on a 'mooch'. Sherlock Holmes had nothing on me!

///

The following morning we sat in the Chancellor's office, and he talked me through the list of priests and staff associated with the cathedral. He gave me a lot of information – far more than I needed, but I let him continue so as to keep my mission covert. I gave him no indication what I was doing or in whom I was expressing an interest.

"Tell me about yourself," I asked. "I love to hear people's histories – I like to hear about people's experiences. How did you come to be a member of the cloth?"

He was eager to tell me as most people are. Nobody is that much interested in other people's stories or their history, so they make the most of someone willing to listen to them. I took notes as he spoke, showing interest, although the information he gave me was of little value.

"Thank you for telling me your story," I said, deceitfully. "That was very interesting. Whoever would've thought from such humble beginnings? You are a very accomplished man." Flattery gets you everywhere.

I looked at the list of personnel he had provided. "I would like to take an example cross-section of the staff associated with the cathedral to interview. Perhaps you are best to advise who might be suitable for this. You have a vast knowledge of the cathedral and those who are assigned to work in this bishopric. I would appreciate your input." Lashings upon lashings of sycophancy.

"That's very kind of you," he replied.

"Not a bit of it – I speak as I find."

"Please can I ask if there is a purpose to interviewing some of these?" he said, pointing at the list.

"Just to get some background information, if that's OK?"

He said it was fine and pointed out four people he thought would be good for interview. He omitted candidate A, so I suggested that for a clearer picture of the bishopric, Candidate A might be of benefit to give his side of things.

"I don't see why not," he said. "Would you like me to arrange the interviews?"

I said I would be very grateful for his kind assistance. I also asked about the possibility of using a small, sparse room for my 'prayers'.

He said there were a lot of small unused rooms inside the cathedral and he would give me access to one of them.

Just as we were leaving, he asked "I don't suppose you've heard how the bishop is doing, have you?" I said I was sorry that I was not privy to that information.

He was a good man to have on my side - friendly, co-operative and obliging.

///

Candidate B was the first of my interviews, which I conducted that same afternoon. The impromptu one I gave the Chancellor was not in my considerations.

"Please come in and take a seat." He sat down. "My name is Father Nicholas and I am a Special Envoy, in partnership with, but not entirely beneath the auspices of the Archbishops' Council. Would you be in agreement to take part in this process in line with this edict?"

"What's it about?" He was quite blunt, but that isn't always a bad thing — rather that than beating around the bush *ad infinitum*.

"We are simply conducting a survey of some bishoprics, taking into consideration the more prominent members of the diocese. Your name has been given to me as 'a man in the know', so to speak. Are you happy for me to proceed?"

"I don't see why not. It's not to do with the funeral, is it?"

"I assume you're alluding to the recent funeral of the nun? No, not all. That is not in my remit. However, I will say that by all accounts, you behaved admirably, intervening and removing the bishop from causing more damage."

"Good. I don't think I want to relive that. I'm not in any trouble, am I?"

"Absolutely not. This is merely an interview. I am not in the business of dishing out disciplinaries."

I sensed he was starting to feel a bit more at ease. Interviews of this nature are so much easier if the interviewee is under the illusion that they are simply having a chat.

We chatted. The man had taken the cloth and was ambitious from the outset. His father was in politics and thirsty for high office, and his son was following his example.

He was likeable, he could be charming, but there was an undercurrent I couldn't quite put my finger on. I couldn't help but wonder why he would have thought he might have been in any trouble.

His was the only interview of the first day. I found the Chancellor and said I'd be back in the morning.

"Good-o," he said. I think that was the first and last time I ever heard somebody use that expression.

///

The second day I conducted two interviews – one in the morning and another in the afternoon. A third had to wait as the person in question was away until the following day.

First interview of the morning was a younger priest who, from his character, was hardly cut out for the priesthood at all.

"Alright, mate!" he said as he entered the room, and plumped himself down on a chair. "What's all this then?"

I explained who I was and my reason for being there.

"Fire away – I'm an open book, me!" He held up a hand and positioned his fingers as though pulling the trigger of a gun. "Bang, bang!"

At least there was no need to try and make this priest (Interviewee C, for those who need to know such things) feel at ease. He was almost supine in his demeanour, laying back in the chair. I fancied offering him a pillow, but resisted the urge to suggest it.

I asked him about his 'calling' and he was quite candid, telling me of his past and how he came to be in the position he found himself in. He reminded me of my brother - an image I tried in vain to extinguish from my thoughts.

He said he would 'have gone Catholic' although brought up an Anglican but hadn't as there wouldn't have been the opportunity to 'do' women. The man made me cringe. However did this man become ordained as a priest? I know I was there to report back, but how I would have enjoyed giving a report about this obnoxious creature! It made sense that he was working in the cathedral setting – no-one would dare to unleash him into a parish on his own!

"Well, thank you so much for giving me a clear picture of this diocese and the part you play in it," I said, lying through my teeth. "I am very much obliged to you."

"No worries, mate," he said. "See yous later, then!"

And out he went, sashaying like a squaddie in a nightclub, making a clucking sound as he went.

He left a bad taste in my mouth, so I went for lunch, sitting on a park bench with a sandwich and time to reflect on the egregious character of the man I had just unfortunately met.

Come the afternoon, I had a much more pleasant encounter with Interviewee D.

He was an older man who had been verger to the cathedral for thirty years or more. He was a cheerful soul, but like Candidate B, thought he might be in trouble. I allayed his fears, but couldn't help but wonder why these two people were so keen to know that they were not in any bother.

There wasn't a lot I needed to know from this individual, so I questioned him about this fear of a reprimand.

"I seem to always be in trouble. Can I speak candidly?"

I assured the verger that everything said between us was highly confidential and wouldn't be shared with anyone.

"The bishop has been a difficult man to work with," he told me. "He's got worse as his...er...um...faculties have deteriorated. He was never an easy man to get along with – quick to chide over the most minor of discrepancies or misdemeanours. Don't get me wrong – I love my job and I am dedicated to God and to the work I do – but this has not been a happy place to work in."

I asked if others of the diocese felt the same.

"I expect so. He has rather put people off from coming here or working here. There is a constant queue of people – good people – who are looking to jump ship and request redeployment. It's a shame."

I chatted more with the man for a while, but there was no point in prolonging the interview.

A picture of the bishopric was forming, yet I had to remember that was not my concern. Perhaps the nominations were best considered in terms of who might be able to right the wrongs going on here.

I hesitated to contact Harry or Eusebius. I needed more information to form a fuller picture of the situation so I could ask the right questions.

Candidate A (who I met in the afternoon) was a very different person from Candidate B. He was a larger, older man who sat down in the chair with an audible 'Oomph!'

I introduced myself with the same introduction I had used with the other interviewees. He was an astute man who questioned my credentials.

"Did you say *Father* Nicholas? Are you a Roman Catholic, then? The only 'Fathers' in the Anglican Church tend be monasterial. Which Order are you affiliated to?"

I told him I was not affiliated to any order. My title was an honorary one.

"I've never in my life met an 'honorary Father'. How did you come by that designation? From which theological college did you graduate?"

I tried to deflect the questioning without success. "My work is confidential, and as such I cannot divulge my own identity. Are you happy to proceed with the interview?"

"Not really, no. I neither know your credentials for you to be able to question me for any cause, nor do I know the purpose of your enquiries. Unless you are able to satisfy me with regards to these concerns, I feel unable to assist you."

"I'm sorry to hear you are not happy with the explanation I have given you. I can assure you there are no improper or indecorous reasons for this interview."

"So why the interview then?"

"It is a simple matter of gathering information about this and other bishoprics. If you are not happy to proceed, this interview can be terminated at your request."

"I request a termination of this interview. Good day to you!"

He eased himself out of the chair and left the room.

I reported back to the Chancellor that it would be opportune to use one of the small rooms he had promised the day before.

He showed me to the room. It contained two chairs, a long bench and a crucifix. I said it was ideal and asked if he could please make sure I wasn't disturbed. "No-one comes up here," he said. "It's all in disuse. You won't be bothered."

I thanked him and closed the door. I put the candle on the bench and the crucifix in my briefcase. I took a slug of 'tea' and evoked Harry. This was becoming easier the more I did it and Harry appeared within a few moments. I failed to evoke Eusebius.

I asked Harry what the problem was in this diocese – why people were not staying on, which is unusual in these circles.

He led me back into the garden (as is his wont) and across to the far side where a fence barred my path. A field of long grass on the other side of the fence came into focus.

I struggled to get Harry to concentrate. Initially I thought it could have been the close proximity of the crucifix. He showed me a large fish head in the arms of a statue. My attention was drawn to one of the hands, which was made of metal.

Harry disappeared without warning. I was left facing this statue which was holding the fish head. I sensed another presence which was not Eusebius. I felt uneasy. I needed the bell to ground me but there was no bell. Rather than being led forward, I was pulled forward, as though struggling through dense mud, against my will.

I asked the spirit his name. He did not answer me - he just continued to pull me forward. I asked the spirit what his name was. He refused to communicate. A shepherd came into view – an up-to-date looking fellow in Wellington boots and a tweed jacket. He held a shepherd's crook, and a broken-down tractor in disrepair was behind him. A sheep dog ran in circles around the shepherd and his tractor. The shepherd whistled loudly in my ear but the dog did not stop running.

The shepherd called the dog again yet it continued to run around and around. The shepherd took his crook and caught the dog by the neck. It yelped and struggled but did not get free from the hook.

The image dissipated, this new spirit left me and Harry led me back to the garden. The head of the fish I had seen on the statue lay on a table in the shed.

I asked Harry who I had just encountered. He showed me an image of the cathedral. Around the cathedral was a wall of fire. A protective spirit? I wasn't sure. I asked Harry if this spirit had a name. No image came. I decided to call it a day and sat and pondered over the images I had just seen.

I knew the bishop's Mitre was created to imitate a fish head – that was quite clear – as was the iron fist – the bishops 'heavy-handedness', if you like. The broken-down tractor was the malfunctioning bishopric and the dog? Maybe someone who was trying to take control but something was holding them back? Was this a good thing or a bad thing? Was someone stopping someone else from causing more break-down of the situation for good or for bad? And who was the shepherd? I wasn't sure.

The Chancellor caught me as I was leaving the cathedral. He told me my final two interviews were planned for the following morning, and I thanked him for arranging them.

"I've spoken to [Candidate A]. He tells me he declined to be interviewed. Is that correct?"

I told him that it was so.

"Is that a problem?" he asked, with concern.

"Not a bit of it," I told him. "It tells me a great deal."

The Chancellor offered me dinner that evening, but I declined. I needed to get matters straight in my head without distraction. There was something amiss, or more likely, afoot, in this place. I just needed to isolate exactly what was going on.

Chapter 21

I had the two remaining interviews lined up for the following morning. Interviewee D was a suffragan bishop and as such liaised and assisted the bishop as and where requested. I could but imagine that in the bishop's current state of mind he was serving a hard task-master. I was intrigued to speak to this man.

"Come in and take a seat, won't you?" I motioned Interviewee D to sit. I introduced myself.

"Happy to help however I can," he said. "God knows we need it – help I mean."

I said I had come to realise that there was something of a 'situation' in this bishopric.

"Situation? Good God man, we're in bleedin' chaos 'ere! He's being going a bit funny for a while now, you know - a bit ga-ga," he informed me.

I guessed he was talking about the bishop. "That must've been very challenging for you," I said.

"You don't know the 'alf!" he said. "He's always been bloody-minded, so it's been difficult to try to rein him in, so to speak."

"I'm under no illusion that these have been difficult times for everybody."

"And he don't treat you right – if you get my drift? He's not what I would call a 'gentleman' – not by any stretch of the imagination."

I nodded and kept quiet so that he would continue, unabated.

"That fiasco at the nun's funeral was just the tip of the iceberg – they won't tell you what other things what's been going on. Sorry to use language, but it's been bloody awful."

"Could you tell me, please?" I asked. "You seem to have the handle on this," speaking in his own parlance.

"Bloody right, an' all! I've seen it all. Given me a right bollocking he has – and not only me, 'e takes it out on anyone what comes into his line of vision."

"In what way?"

"Swears at 'em; shouts at 'em; calls 'em names – you've never 'eard the like. It'd turn your blood cold."

I sat musing, rubbing my chin with my thumb and forefinger. "From your very vivid description, would it be fair to say he is out of control?"

"Out of control? The man's a bleedin' liability. If he were a 'orse, you wouldn't put no money on him."

"Thank you for being so open with me. I appreciate your forthrightness."

"Yeah, well, speak as I find."

"Perhaps you could tell me what your current duties are?"

He explained how he tried to organise the bishop's calendar; made phone calls on his behalf; got him to appointments on time and had taken to writing letters on the bishop's behalf. Hopefully, his written English was an improvement on his spoken form.

"Do you find other members of this diocese are helpful, or would you say they are more of a hindrance? You can speak to me in total confidence. What you tell me will go no further." He sat with a look on his face as if to say he doubted my confidentiality.

"Well," he said, "I'm not saying he's a total pain in the.... neck, 'cos he 'ain't. But there's someone trying to put the kibosh on things. He meddles – know what I mean? I mean, I know my onions and I think I do a good job, but because I'm not stuck up like some of 'em, they think I'm not capable. I'm rough and ready – I know that. But I'd rather be like I am than walk around with me nose in the air like everyone smells like...something not very nice.

"I'm not saying it's all of 'em, cos it's not, but one person sticks 'is oar in where it's really not wanted." He pointed to a photograph in a row of photographs on the wall. "'im!" he said with some vehemence. He indicated Candidate A. "Thinks 'e runs the place, but 'e's just a know-it-all busybody. It was 'im told the bishop to conduct the nun's funeral and told 'im 'e should preside over the proceedings. I tried to stop 'im – the bishop, that is - but 'e weren't 'aving none of it. 'Can I remind you that I am the bishop and I give the instructions. Now go about your business – I know what I'm doing!' That's what 'e said just because of this meddling old goat. This is what I've been dealing with – it's been an absolute nightmare, I can tell ya!"

Interviewee D continued to tell me in his colourful way of the problems he and the bishopric were experiencing.

He was not an erudite man, but his heart was in the right place. My suspicions were that Candidate A was well-meaning, but was perhaps speaking out of turn while the bishop still held office.

On his way out, Interviewee D said, "I'll stand ya a pint if you're free later?" I thanked him for his kind gesture, but I explained that I would be busy.

"As you will," he said, "but the offer's there if ya change ya mind."

///

I still had Interviewee E to meet, and I grabbed a bite of lunch before meeting her. The interviewee was housekeeper to the bishop.

She was a charming and quiet woman who had taken care of the bishop for twenty years or more. She had an air of subservience about her and clearly had some deep-rooted feelings for the bishop. I couldn't see that there was anything controlling or untoward in what she felt was a vocation.

Bizarrely, but in a gesture of her care, she gave me a slice of cherry and coconut cake which was the bishop's favourite.

///

This left me with the following evidence:

Candidate A had refused to be interviewed, so I did not have his testimony to consider – only third-hand information, which was not flattering. His reported high-handedness might prove to be a continuation rather than a resolution to the problems in the bishopric.

Candidate B was charming and ambitious. Something (I did not know what) made me reticent to suggest him as being suitable for the role of the bishop. I needed to delve deeper.

Interviewee C was an obnoxious beast of a man.

Interviewee D was what you might call a 'rough diamond'. He was a kind-hearted man who was struggling to cope in difficult circumstances.

Interviewee E – the housekeeper - was a kindly soul, who had dedicated her years (and possibly her heart) to the retiring bishop.

Once I had established what was causing me to doubt the suitability of Candidate B for the position, I would be able to produce the report which was expected of me. It was going to be challenging to produce any kind of an unbiased account and not express an opinion.

I wanted to reconnect with the unnamed spirit I had encountered the day before.

I hid myself away in the little room I was borrowing. Again, I put the crucifix into my bag and took a sip of the 'Magister's tea.'

First to make contact was Eusebius. I asked Eusebius how I could contact the spirit protector of the cathedral, which I wasn't able to do without knowing the spirit's name. Harry joined in, and as usual led me through the garden and into the shed. I looked out of the window in the shed and all the garden was grey – there were no colours at all. The grass and sky were grey as were the flower beds and the fields beyond. "Is his name 'Grey'?" I asked. "Or Graham?" Colour came back to everything in my field of view.

I thanked Harry. I made preparations to communicate with Graham. Eusebius showed me a briefcase, with something trying to get out of it. I took the crucifix out of my bag and put it back on the wall. Perhaps such things were of some importance to Graham. Maybe not the presence of the crucifix, but maybe he didn't like change – I was unsure.

Harry led me back to the shed in the garden and on the table was a teapot. It seemed necessary to take another slug of the Magister's tea, which I did.

I waited for what seemed a very long time looking at the teapot. Eventually, Harry led me out into the garden, then all of a sudden, without warning I was stood on a sandy beach looking out to sea. This was not Harry – I could sense Graham.

I asked Graham what it was about Candidate B I was uneasy about. The wind picked up and the sea became choppy – rising and falling. I could feel water on my feet – the tide was coming in. A tall ship came into view far in to the distance. It drew closer to the beach and looked likely to be beached. Candidate B was stood at the helm holding a pair of binoculars. Seamen ran around the deck bailing out water, tethering the sails. But Candidate B was not looking out for danger – he was viewing a row of deckchairs on a pier, jutting out to sea. As chaos surrounded him, he climbed into a rowing boat and rowed himself to the pier, heading towards the row of deckchairs.

The image changed, again unexpectedly. There was no gradual change in imagery like there was with Harry or Eusebius. Graham was more direct in his approach. Candidate B was stood in front of a fence. He was surrounded by beautiful blooms, but different flowers were blossoming on the far side of the fence. He was stretching and reaching for the flowers that he couldn't quite grasp.

I had my answer that Candidate B did not want the life he had as a man of the cloth. He was aiming for something different – he was ambitious, but not for a life in the Church. His ambitions were more worldly. I questioned why he should have considered a life in God's service rather than entering politics as his father had.

I was being led to another place. I needed to stop this session, but was not able to do so. The image of the teapot came into view again. I didn't want to take another sip of the Magister's tea, but I was being pressured to do so. I had the answer I needed, but one of the spirits had something he wanted to show me. Should I stop the session or continue as I was being led? From what I could make out, I was going to be shown something important, so against my better judgment, I took another small sip of tea.

This was not one of my known spirits. I asked the spirit for his identity. He showed me a fully equipped gymnasium. 'Jim' - that was clear. The Head Office came into view, surrounded by soldiers with guns. A cannon was pointed at the front door; it was being loaded and a fuse had been lit. Dozens of cannonballs were on the ground ready to be used. Head Office was under attack.

I ended the session promptly, but I'd had three sips of the Magister's tea and it took time for me to refocus. There was a knock on the door to my room. The Chancellor was stood there apologising for disturbing me. I said there was no need to apologise.

"I've received a rather urgent phone call," he said. "A bit of a cryptic message, I'm afraid. The caller didn't give their name. The message was simple – 'Return to the MAD-house urgently!' Does that make any sense to you?

I said it did. I thanked him for all his assistance, and drove directly to Head Office.

Chapter 22

The administrator took me directly to the Magister Princeps (the Chief Magister) – a man I had not met previously.

"Thank you for coming so promptly. We have a serious issue."

The Magister Princeps was younger than I had imagined him to be. He came over as being humourless, but the gravity of the situation we were in probably gave him this demeanour.

"I apologise for asking James to interrupt you." (I assumed he meant 'Jim)'. "Thank you for following his lead."

I said it was no imposition. "What is the issue?" I asked, keen to find out what the problem was and whether I was the problem or the solution. I hoped the latter.

"Some years ago, you attended a course in Cambridge, is that correct?"

I said it was – I had been on two courses held in Cambridge.

"Yes – it's the first course which is concerning me." This was the first course I went on when I first met Ignatius. "Do you recall a young man on that course, from Aberdeen?" This was the Scottish lad who had left the course half way through it.

I told the Magister Princeps I remembered him.

"Well, he's been causing quite a stir and has become something of a thorn in our side."

The Scottish lad had not continued with his study of the Dark Arts. Instead he enrolled in a course of journalism, and in that capacity he had been writing numerous articles about the dangers of cult and occult organisations. His work was gaining some followers and he had come to the attention of some prominent people. His personal experiences of our organisation were taken as gospel, and yet were far from the actual truth. However, his private 'insider' knowledge was being taken seriously.

"We have come under the scrutiny by several leaders in different fields and our influence is being questioned."

I said that we only influence those who request our influence.

"There is a certain Canon (he said his name, but I am unable to divulge it) who has taken it upon himself to undermine this organisation and to question our services. He has intimated that we have ulterior motives, stating we are aiming for high office. He is not accepting any of our explanations. He has requested an assembly of Church leaders and ourselves to discuss the impending and imminent dangers our organisation poses to the Church and to society as a whole."

I told the Magister Princeps the absurdity of the Canon's claims. He asked me to tell him the exact nature of the Scottish lad's experience when on the course, and what my impression of him was.

I told him the circumstances of him leaving the course – of course, he had left before finding out exactly what our relationship is to the spirit world and had not had enough time nor experience to play witness to anything to which he could bear testimony. I refrained from telling the Magister Princeps about the Scottish lad being the victim of our very naughty 'Copy Cat Game'.

"A council of Magisters has been convened. We have unanimously voted that you are the best able to address the assembly of Church leaders and to answer their questions. Your experience with members of the clergy gives you a distinct advantage over anyone else amongst us to speak for us and to answer with utmost diplomacy, any questions which could be put to us. I would be interested to hear your thoughts on the matter."

I said I was flattered that the organisation held me and my abilities in such high esteem, but I was unsure if I was truly the right person for the job.

"Your reticence is understandable. To take this role, you are in danger of being exposed and you could be put 'on the spot' so to speak. I don't want or expect an answer from you now. I know you are not a person to take anything lightly or without due care and attention, and that you would give this task the most careful consideration. What I would like you to do would be to take a couple of days here with us, to mull over and discuss with myself, or other Magisters or your spirits any misgivings or questions you might have. Would that be acceptable?"

I said it was a reasonable proposition. And if I refused?

"We would think nothing less of you. Your work has been far beyond anything we might have expected of you – that would not change. But - and it is a big but here - the organisation itself is in danger of not being able to continue. Whether your present position would still be available after this period of trial would be in doubt – as it would be for any or all of us. If you are happy to proceed with your deliberations...?"

I said I was.

"Excellent. I have assigned you Room Six on the second floor. The administrator will direct you to your room. We eat at seven in the refectory. If you need anything at all before then, please ask the administrator. The house, the administrator and the Magisters are at your disposal."

I sat in my room and considered the path I had taken to reach this position. From stacking the shelves in the minimarket on the Sandling Roa to my interview with my Magister, my journey as an adept and now Magister Legatus and being asked to bear this great responsibility – how it had come to this was something of a mystery to me. Had it all stemmed from Gerald's blessing? Is that when my journey truly began? It was inconceivable that an ordinary Maidstone boy had reached so high in his chosen profession. As I thought those words it occurred to me – I had not *chosen* this profession. In a way I did not yet understand, the profession had chosen me.

There was still two hours until dinner, so I sat and wrote my report from my previous engagement.

I, Magister Legatus Liberius, of the Magisterial Association of Divination (sine officio) do solemnly swear to the following report as being good and true, sine praeiudicio (without bias).

The purpose of this report is to assess potential replacement bishops for the bishopric of (sorry – I can't tell you the seat of the bishopric).

Two nominees for the position have been suggested, and it has been my assignment to ascertain the suitability or incongruity of the said contenders.

The bishopric was found to be in a profound state of disorder. The current bishop is in poor health, and as such has been unable to take part in these proceedings.

It became apparent through questioning candidates and non-candidates that the bishopric has been in a state of flux for some period of time. This has resulted in some clergical and some non-clergical personnel leaving the diocese. Retention of staff has been difficult. However, some staff members have been found to be loyal to the outgoing bishop, regardless of the problems the diocese has encountered.

The first of the two candidates put forward for promotion is the younger of the two nominees. He is an ambitious young man. However, I found that he is not settled in his chosen field and is likely to find an alternative occupation. He is not loyal to the Church – only to his own advancement.

The second of the candidates is an older man who has been loyal to the Church and to the outgoing bishop for many years. While he is not an easy man to interact with his heart is without doubt in the 'right place'. He has the propensity to be stubborn and tenacious, and in the wrong circumstances could be considered heavy-handed. Other members of this bishopric could be considered to be in need of some discipline, and this candidate would be in the right position to address inappropriate behaviour where necessary. Although not a particularly popular man, facing the challenges the position *requires, this man would be able to cope with those challenges and exercise some control.*

I would like to thank all those who assisted me in this assignment. I am particularly grateful to the Canon Chancellor whose friendly, co-operative manner was a great help in the execution of this project.

I put the report in an envelope, sealed it with a wax seal and took it down to dinner, handing it to the Magister Princeps as I passed his place at the table.

After dinner, I retired to my room to consider the new proposition.

Chapter 23

After breakfast the next morning, the Magister Princeps asked me to join him in his office. He asked if I had any questions about the impending assignment.

"Just a couple of hundred," I answered him. He raised a smile for the first time. Even over dinner he had sat without any kind of facial expression.

"Name them," he said, simply.

"Would I be there alone, or would there be other Magisters to assist me in case of questions arising to which I don't know the answer?"

"I'll be there, but you will be the nominated negotiator. Other Magisters will not be present – we don't want this to look like an envoy!"

"Do we know who is likely to be invited to the assembly?"

"The short answer to that is a 'no', I'm afraid. However, I will ask for a list of attendees prior to the assembly taking place. Is there a reason for asking?"

"I need to know who is present to adjust my answers accordingly. The last thing I would want to do would be to offend anyone present."

"Forever the ambassador," he replied. "I'm sorry to say that just by your presence you will be likely to offend some attendees. You will be playing to a hostile audience. Anything else?"

"I was wondering if I could get hold of any of the articles this Scottish lad has written. If I know exactly what he has said, it will be easier to have some answers ready."

"Good thinking," he said. "I'll get those for you."

"Do we know when this is likely to take place? There's some training I want to request – if there's time."

"What training?" he asked.

"Cold-reading." My Magister had taught me a lot about how to read people's deportment, but there was a lot more I needed to know – how people walk, how they hold their hands, and all that kind of thing. By being able to read my critics, I would be better placed to respond to them in the correct manner.

"I know a doctor – retired now – but he has helped us occasionally in the past – a very clever and astute man. I'll give him a call. You might have to go to him, though. I don't think he's so mobile these days. As for timing, the Canon is pressing for next week."

"That's soon. There are some questions I have for one of my spirit guides. Can I ask if I'm OK to give you a definite answer a little later, please?"

"No, problem," he said. "I'll get hold of the doctor and see if he can help you. I'll try and obtain those written articles you have requested. Any more questions, please don't hesitate to ask. I might not know the answers, but I'll help all I can."

As I was leaving, he said "Sorry – spirit room is Room Twelve. If you need me or any of the other Magisters to assist, let me know."

I thanked him. I had become accustomed to communing with the spirits on my own, so no assistance was necessary. I needed to get more information about the scene Harry had shown me of a room with an audience, when we first made contact.

I found the room and made contact with Harry. Eusebius joined in without being asked, but it was of no matter.

I asked Harry about the scene he had showed me previously. As ever, he first led me into the garden and then on into the shed in the corner. I turned to look out through the shed window. An enormous abyss opened up on the garden side of the window. The hole was deep – from where I stood, I could not see the bottom of it. Rocks and turf were tumbling into the hole. The sides of the pit were steep and unnavigable. Flames shot up from somewhere in the base of the pit, not in any particular pattern. I was on the brink of an abyss. How easy it would be to fall in to it. Facilis descensus averno.

My focus moved away from the window and the abyss to the table inside the shed. Strewn across the table were a pile of documents and a Bible. A picture of a kangaroo was in amongst the papers as was a picture of a noose. I was likely to be facing a 'kangaroo court'. The clergy had already come to a conclusion and I was going to have to fight their preconceived judgments. I asked the spirits how best to fight my corner. My focus centred on the Bible. Outside, a strange boxing match was taking place – one candle was fighting another candle. The candles dissolved until there were just the flames jousting at one another. I was to fight fire with fire!

I knew better than to ask the likely outcome of the confrontation – spirits can only guide, not foretell.

I regained my lucidity due to a tap on the door. The Magister Princeps was good to his word and had arranged for me to visit the doctor he had told me about.

///

First thing in the morning, I took the two-hour drive to see the doctor. I would give the Magister Princeps my decision about the assembly when I returned, either one way or another.

The doctor was living out his retirement years in a large, modern detached house. His wife answered the door and told me the doctor was expecting me and to go through to the lounge where he was waiting.

The doctor was sitting in a wide armchair in the bay window at the far side of the room. He greeted me without getting out of his chair – it was apparent that as was anticipated, his mobility was impaired.

"Forgive me if I don't get up," he said, smiling. "I'm not so good on my feet these days. Would you prefer tea or coffee?"

I said I'd prefer coffee and he called out to his wife Doris, who came back into the room. "Bring us some tea, would you please, dear?" I assumed he had misheard me saying 'coffee', but it was of no concern.

"So, it's cold-reading, is it?" he asked.

I said that was what I hoped he was going to help me with.

"I would rather you had asked for tea," he said.

I asked why.

"You drink too much coffee – you are on the verge of becoming anaemic. Your thumb nails," he said, pointing at my hands. "See the convex of your right thumb nail – this is a sign of mild anaemia, probably due to drinking too much coffee. Try changing to tea. You are also leaning a little to the left when you walk. Some spinal exercises should right that, and if caught soon enough, will prevent a multitude of spinal problems later in life."

The man amazed me with these simple but effective diagnoses.

Doris brought in the teas.

"Now watch as Doris leaves. It's OK, Doris, you get along. Watch her gait – how she walks. What do you see?"

I said that she walked steadily and slowly and that her shoulders were a little hunched.

"And what of her arms? How was she holding her arms as she walked? Was her neck bent or upright? Were her feet splayed or in line with her shoulders? It is not only the legs we look at when we watch someone walk – we take into consideration their entire body – all body parts are incorporated into the motion of walking – which is why it is such a healthy form of exercise – the whole body is exercised. That might do your impending back problems some good."

He explained that any doctor worth his salt sits the patient as far from the door of the surgery as possible, to glean as much from the patient's walk as they can. "Half of any doctor's diagnosis should be taken just from the gait of the patient as they come into the surgery. It's just as important as what the patient tells the doctor is wrong with them.

"You came in here not ten minutes ago, and I could tell from your walk that you have confidence but were nervous. Why you should be nervous about meeting me, is anyone's guess. You looked straight ahead and looked directly at me. You didn't look around the room, but at me directly. This shows a forthrightness and confidence. What gave your game away as to your nervousness was that your hands were clenched as you walked, and you didn't allow your arms a natural swing as you came over to me. Now, go back over to the door and cross the room towards me again – this time, make sure your hands aren't clenched into fists, and allow your arms to swing naturally."

I did as he asked. "That's better – you're not looking so nervous. Now do it again, this time making your thumbs more prominent – let them stick out. Do that and without sitting down, shake my hand."

The doctor's insight was staggering. He took me through handshaking – the right ways and wrong ways of doing what to all intents and purposes you would think is a simple manoeuvre. He taught me how to tell a lot about the person whose hand you are shaking.

"Tell me if you have any questions as we progress, or if you are not sure how to interpret different scenarios. Right – you have now developed a good and confident walk and handshake. Now, stand up and sit down again, please."

I did as he bid me. "Don't move a muscle! Tell me without looking, what position are your feet in; how you are holding your hands and are you leaning forwards or backwards? Before you tell me that, close your eyes, please, but don't move from the position you are sitting in now."

I closed my eyes. "Right – tell me how I am sitting. Are my feet flat on the floor? Are my legs slightly apart or far apart or are they crossed?"

I had learned a lot from doing the 'Copy Cat Game' with Ignatius, but admitted I hadn't really been paying attention. I knew his feet were flat on the floor, but I couldn't tell him the position of his legs or any other parts of his body.

"That's usual – you'll have to learn to take note of the very smallest detail immediately when you first meet someone. Now, how are you sitting?"

I told him the details he asked me.

"I appreciate you are in a learning posture presently, but with a few tweaks we can make you look far more confident and also give you an air of honesty. If you are to speak and be believed, you need to exude an air of truthfulness – even if you're lying through your teeth. We'll do this exercise standing and sitting. Hand posture is crucial to this as are the position of the feet."

These were difficult lessons to master. I told the doctor about how I had been taught to use voice tone and pitch to give confidence in what I was saying. He nodded. "Tell me what you've just told me again. This time, use your hands and your feet in tandem with voice tone and pitch. How about – try telling me it's raining outside, although it's a bright sunny day?"

This was a good exercise. "With good practice, you can have anyone believe anything you say. But a word of warning here – forget one small thing and the whole image can be destroyed – you will be found out. Although largely subconscious, we pick up on lies very quickly. This is why police put family and friends in front of the cameras when someone is missing or murdered – no matter what words people say, inflection and deportment tell far more than words ever could. Right, try this again – tell me what you think of this learning exercise so far."

I laughed. I had no need to lie – this training was far better than my expectation.

"Thank you for your honesty – I think," he said, smiling. "Right, now we need to concentrate on attack. When we under attack – verbally not physically, we need to fight like with like without saying a single word. To combat a verbal attack, we do not use words – that just creates argument. There are much simpler ways to win an argument. I want you to tell me something – anything – the subject of the argument doesn't matter. Tell me about your journey here this morning. Watch my eyes and my hands as you tell me."

I did as he asked. "I left Head Office this morning at around eight o'clock." (His eyes looked up to the right); "It was a clear run except for some roadworks which held me up for a good twenty minutes." (His eyes looked down to the left and he folded his arms); "I followed the signs to this village," (he unfolded his arms and leaned forward) "and I arrived here at just gone ten o'clock." (He momentarily closed his eyes and left out a gentle sigh). I could see exactly what he was doing – he was giving the impression I was telling a load of lies, even though I was telling the truth.

"You know, reacting like this – silently – can enrage your opponent" he said, "and once enraged, their argument is lost. You can't argue effectively if you lose your temper."

Lying, telling the truth and argument carried on until lunchtime. Doris brought lunch in to us and we sat at the table. "Eat your dinner, then we'll talk about eating and drinking – but enjoy your meal first."

We had already discussed about sitting on a stage in front of an audience. "Practice sitting with your right leg at right angles to the floor and your left leg outstretched, but not to its full potential." I had already forgotten to sit in this position and corrected my posture. "That's better," he said, "let's eat!"

We ate lunch and then resumed our training. Eating and drinking were difficult manoeuvres to master, in particular standing, taking sips of water as you do when in front of an audience. "Remember not to rest your free arm on the lectern when sipping water. You look slovenly. Arm by your side, take a sip of water with the other hand and look over the top of the glass. You don't want to look boss-eyed every time you take a sip. You don't need to look at the glass. You will intuitively know how to bring the glass to your lips without looking at it. I have to say though, best practice would be to not use the lectern at all – you can look like you're delivering a sermon. It would be best to stand in front of the lectern – you can still put the water on it and any notes you might have. You can reach round to access them, should you need them."

This made perfect sense.

"OK, let's deal with attacks – verbal of course. I don't pretend to know much about your profession, but I do know you use symbols for various herbs and the such, and there are inverted symbols which produce an opposite reaction. That's right, isn't it?"

213

I said that in short that was correct, although sometimes an inverted symbol can produce the symptoms of the potion, without actually becoming real.

"Like a placebo?"

"Yes, something like that."

"Good. We can do the same with hostile postures – we can negate them by using our own postures and gestures. An attack can be negated."

He showed me some examples. To give an impression of how this works, he sat with his arms folded and his feet behind him under the chair. This is a hostile gesture and also one of self-protection – in this posture you are defending yourself and also in a position of conflict. Rather like using a shield as a weapon. That's as well as I can explain it, anyway. The gesture and posture I could use in response would be to show the hostile element that I am no threat, and also give the person the ability to drop his guard of self-preservation. Once the hostile threat has been banished, it is easier to get someone to be on your side and less confrontational. This combined with the honesty postures can turn an enemy (or potential enemy) into not necessarily a friend, but non-hostile and more open to listen to your point of view.

The doctor showed me similar techniques for dealing with someone who is overly confident (making them doubt themselves), the crowd-pleasers (to make them unpopular) and the bigoted (to make them more understanding). This was like learning a foreign language with all the complexities of syntax and grammar.

"We have covered a lot of ground," the doctor said. "It's not easy and there is so much more I would like to show you. I'll just tell you a few medical diagnosis techniques, more out of interest than of any practical use, but you never know, do you?"

I said I was grateful for anything he could show me. He taught me how to recognise a diabetic, underlying heart conditions, pulmonary diseases, gastrointestinal disorders and a confused mind. I did not know that so much could be understood without a single word being said.

"There's a lot more," he told me. "But these need closer examination of eyes, hands and ears, but these are not of much use if viewing somebody at a distance."

He continued. "I know our time here is nearing to an end, but two things before you go. The first is simple – by looking at your hands you are destined for high office, trust me. Your powers of communication will take you there – I hope that what you have learned today will add to the great skills you have already perfected. The second thing I have to ask you is a rather peculiar request – I only hope you will be able to oblige me."

I told him that if it was within my power to do so, I was at his service.

"My wife," he said, "loves anything to do with the Dark Arts. I mean – she doesn't practice or anything like that, but she loves natural cures and healing stones and all that malarky. She enjoys watching the sunrise at Stonehenge on the Summer Equinox – you know – white magic she calls it."

I said I understood. "I suppose you mean fortune tellers, as well – that kind of thing."

"Exactly so," he answered. "Knowing you were coming here today, my wife was quite excited and asked if she could speak to you for five minutes. I said I would ask you, but I know how secretive those of your profession can be."

"I would be very happy to do so."

"Thank you so much – it would mean a lot to her. She's in the conservatory – perhaps what you say to her should remain private. Please feel free to find her through there." He pointed to the door.

I found Doris in the conservatory, knitting. "Thank you for that wonderful lunch," I said. "You did us proud – I don't think I could eat for a week!"

Doris smiled a wide smile – an almost joyous smile.

"I'm so glad you enjoyed it," she said. "It's not often we get visitors these days and certainly not one as esteemed as you!"

I thanked her for such kind words. "The doctor has intimated that you would like to ask me something. Please feel free to ask – I will be very pleased to answer you, if I can."

"That's very kind of you," she said. "You might think me a silly old fool, but I have always had an interest in other-worldly things, but have never taken part in anything myself. I just want to experience something for myself – something personal to me. I've no idea what that might be, though.

Would you be able to do something just for me? It would mean so much."

I said I would be happy to help her, but would need my case from the room. I collected my case. "Is everything alright?" the doctor asked. I told him everything was fine. I would be a few minutes.

Doris was sitting on the edge of her chair in expectation.

"When I was a very young boy," I told her, "a family friend bestowed a blessing on me. That blessing has followed me my entire life, and I want to share this with you." I took a phial of the 'Magister's tea' from my case and a second phial of bitter water.

"Do you need me to sit or stand?" she asked.

"I want you to sit," I instructed her. "When you put on a dab of perfume, you put your finger on the end of the bottle and tip it onto your finger. I need you to do this with this elixir and put just a tiny drop on the end of your tongue for me. Don't be alarmed, but you might feel a little light-headed. You will be perfectly safe." I did this to give her a feeling of euphoria without any danger. "Please lift your hands in the air, as though in a position of surrender." She did as I asked. "Once you have taken the drop of this elixir, put your hands back into this position. I am going to anoint you. I will need you to stay calm as I do so. Are you alright for me to go ahead?"

"Very much so," she said. "I can't think when I've ever been quite so excited."

"Please take a drop of the elixir and we will proceed."

She did as I asked and raised her hands back into the position of surrender. I spoke a few words of Latin – just a short Latin poem and as I did so, I dabbed a dot of liquid from the phial of bitter water on her left hand, then her right hand and then on her forehead. Doris looked upwards with her eyes closed in a mild state of euphoria. I then recited the Flags, Flax, Fodder and Frig blessing I had learned some years previously, with my right hand on the top of her head.

"Arise, sister of the Dark Arts, and know you have been blessed." Doris stood up and beamed at me with a radiant smile. A small tear ran down her cheek and she hugged me. I guessed she was still under the mild influence of the Magister's tea.

She looked into my eyes and said "I cannot tell you how happy you have made me. Thank you so much."

I told her she was more than welcome and squeezed her hand.

I visited the couple a few times in the years to come, becoming great friends. I could relax with the doctor and his wife and whenever I did so, I felt I was at home.

I returned to Head Office.

Chapter 24

I had only been back at the MAD House an hour when the Magister Princeps knocked on my door.

"How did you get on?" he asked. "Good, isn't he?"

I said he was fantastic and I had learned a lot. More than a lot – I had learned more than I ever could have imagined.

"I'm pleased to hear it," he said. "The housekeeper is asking if you have any washing? I don't suppose you've been able to get home for a while."

I had a suitcase full of dirty laundry. I hadn't been back to Maidstone for a few weeks.

"Just leave it outside your room – the housekeeper will sort it out for you. Join me downstairs for a coffee when you're ready. There are a few things I would like to go through with you."

I said I would be down in about five or ten minutes when I had sorted out the clothes I needed cleaning.

I found the Magister Princeps in the lounge reading a newspaper.

"I'm glad you found the doctor to be useful. He has done a lot for us over the years. We did him a favour some years ago and he's never forgotten it. He refuses to take a penny for his time or expertise."

I said what a wondrous help he had been.

"Right. I'm not one to mince my words - have you made a decision about the assembly?"

219

I said I wasn't exactly happy to do it, but I was prepared to do so.

"Excellent!" he said. "What are you going to wear – for the assembly, I mean?"

It wasn't something to which I'd given a moment's thought. I was more concerned with how I would hold my arms while standing in front of the lectern rather than the clothes I was going to wear. "Casual, but not scruffy, I suppose."

"Mmm," he pondered. "Perhaps a suit – but we don't want you to look too smart – not extravagant or well-to-do, just ordinary but professional. Magister Cornelius will run you into town this afternoon. There's a tailor we use there – he's very good. I'll give you a note to hand to him – he'll know what would be the best kind of suit to wear."

I thanked the Magister.

"You could do with a hair-cut as well. We'll kill two birds with one stone and get you to the barber's as well. Is there anything else you can think of you might need?"

I couldn't think of anything.

"I've asked for the articles you need to see – they should be here tomorrow. We've got a couple of days to prepare."

"When is the assembly going to take place?" I asked.

"Tuesday at six. A conference room has been booked near to Westminster Hall. I've booked hotel rooms for us for that night – it might be late when we finish. If we get there about lunchtime, we'll have a few hours to sort ourselves out and get something to eat. We don't want to be facing the firing squad on an empty stomach."

I laughed – perhaps he did have a sense of humour after all.

"Great. Right. I'll get Magister Cornelius to give you a knock after lunch. Harry's your guiding spirit, isn't he?"

I said that Harry and Eusebius helped me.

"It might be worth asking them to run through some potential questions you might be asked, and ask their guidance for some appropriate answers. They'll be able to guide you about what to say and what not to say. Eusebius will also be able to give you some good Biblical throw-backs. It's always good to fight fire with fire."

///

Suited and booted with a fresh haircut, I felt so much better about the impending assembly.

The rest of the day was spent communing with Eusebius. The information he gave me was worth its weight in gold. Harry showed me some calming techniques.

The Magister Princeps gave me some useful advice – "What is two plus two?" Of course, I answered 'four'. "Let's try that again. This time, give me the appearance you are carefully considering your answer. What is two plus three?"

I paused. The doctor had shown me how to look like I was thinking deeply. "The answer is five," I answered. "However, I have seen from various sources that if converted from logarithms to antilogarithms, the answer would be closer to

221

five point one." What I gave as an answer was an example of me telling a lie, but in such a way that it could be believed.

"And some people questioned my choice of spokesman for this assignment. Well done – you're going to bag this one!"

I sincerely hoped so.

The requested articles written by the Scottish ex-Novitiate came in the post next morning. I spent the bulk of the day studying them. From what I could perceive, he had joined numerous organisations, then left them and had written grotesque critiques about each one. Ours was not the exception. Reading these pieces gave me a good insight into the mind of the author. He was after recognition, a good founding in journalism and a feeling of power over the organisations he had infiltrated. He was most scathing of the followers of Sun Myung Moon, colloquially known as the Moonies. I pitied the members of that organisation for his unrestrained attack. Rightly or wrongly – no-one deserved such an appalling critique involving some well-meaning individuals.

///

We arrived in London at Tuesday lunchtime. We found our hotel and made sure we knew how to get to the Conference Hall ready for that evening.

A message had been left for us in the hotel reception – a paper listing the expected attendees. Fifty-four delegates in all were expected to attend. Most were from the Anglican or Roman Catholic Churches, then there were a couple of Baptists, a

Methodist, a representation from the Salvation Army, two Rabbis, and an independent preacher - who offered no information about his denomination. Evangelists, Pentecostals, Jehovah's Witnesses and the Church of the Latter-Day Saints were not represented.

We lunched, had afternoon tea and then prepared for the evening's proceedings. We arrived at the Hall half an hour before the assembly was due to begin. I arranged the area around the lectern as the doctor had advised – with a chair next to it (which was to be mine), and one to the right away from it (which was for the Magister Princeps). This gave a clear message that the Magister Princeps (I nearly wrote 'was not the one on trial' (!) was not there to answer questions.

A jug of water was already in place on the lectern. We were set and ready for the impending onslaught. We had decided I wasn't to wear a tie – it looked too formal. I put my jacket on the back of my chair but did not roll up my shirt sleeves – I didn't want to look like I was spoiling for a fight.

First through the door was the Canon who had arranged the assembly. I went to greet him with an outstretched hand.

The words he first spoke were to set the tone for the whole of the proceedings. He declined to shake my hand with the words "He who toucheth pitch shall be defiled."

I finished the Apocryphal quote for him (as coached by Eusebius) "And he that hath fellowship with a proud man shall be like unto him."

He pursed his lips, told me to get out of his way, took a chair out of the front row of the audience, and placed it near to mine at the front of the auditorium.

Perhaps I was wrong to answer him as I did, but fighting fire with fire might be the only way to get through to this man – and probably the rest of the assembly. "Don't worry," the Magister Princeps whispered to me. "All gas and no substance."

Very quietly, the Magister Princeps said to me "For the purpose of this occasion, refer to me as 'Stephanus'. Best not to look too hierarchical." I agreed to do as he asked and decided at the same time to simply refer to myself as Liberius.

The rest of the attendees trickled in. Some knew each other, others sat quietly alone. Most were dressed in their uniforms of office (if they had one) – I suppose to give the appearance of being in authority. I remember telling the vicar in East London to do exactly the same thing.

The hubbub of the arriving participants subsided and the Canon took his place behind the lectern, looking very much as if he was just about to give an hour-long sermon. He had copious notes, most of which were probably pure waffle.

I watched him intently as he prepared to speak. And speak he did...

Chapter 25

"Thank you all for agreeing to come to this assembly. We come from different backgrounds and all have varying agendas, but one thing is certain – brothers, friends, comrades-in-arms - we are here to disparage the infidel!" He pointed at me directly, his hand close to my face. Good Lord, the man could be dramatic! He spoke with such vehemence, droplets of spit were clearly visible coming from his mouth.

I used the facial characteristics the doctor had taught me to give the impression the man was not of sound mind. Whether anybody noticed my expressions or were more focussed on the tantruming Canon, I was unsure. I cast my eyes to upper right and slowly closed my eyelids.

The theatrical Canon continued his monologue. "There is an evil amongst us, friends, there is an evil rising up and we, with the help of the living God, will dispel this menace from God and His Holy Church! This is not a time to sit and do nothing – those halcyon days have come to an end. We must stand up against this paganism – this...this...this Godless heathen, who is corrupting our youth and taking advantage of the indifference of this modern society to promote and propagate his sinful lust for evil! There is no doubt, no doubt at all – believe me brothers - Satan is unleashed and walking among us!" He turned and pointed directly at me again, shaking his hand and with a snarl etched onto his face.

Good Heavens! The man deserved an Oscar for this performance! I was watching the audience as he spat out his words. This looked like an everyday rhetoric to them – a fire and brimstone preacher, reminding the Godless of the ravages of Hell. The best way I could describe the look on their faces was 'indifferent' – like a man casually eating an ice cream as his roller-coaster plummets into hidden depths.

To be honest, if this God-fearing Canon was likely to enter Heaven, I would definitely prefer to go to the other place.

He banged some papers onto the palm of his hand. "Here is the proof of this pestilence! An account of this man and his evil ways – communing with demons, cavorting with the devil, making a mockery of our Lord and Saviour. The scripture is clear – 'Thou shalt not suffer a witch to live'! It's here, in the Bible as plain as day!" He waved a copy of the Bible around – highly histrionic but actually serving no purpose other than to waft air about.

"And hereupon I make a stand against this malicious evil. 'Let the heathen be judged in Thy sight. Put them in fear, O Lord: That the nations may know themselves to be but men.'"

Written as poetry, the Canon made the Psalms sound more like a call to war. He went on seemingly *ad nauseam*.

"Take care, my friends, take great care. Arm yourselves against the words of this evildoer. The Lord shall prevail!" He raised his Bible high in the air again as though it was a banner and he a flagbearer. He coughed a little and then sat down, mopping his brow.

My time had come. I stood to my feet and surveyed my audience. I stood as I had planned in front of the lectern. I turned to face the Canon who was struggling to catch his breath from his tirade of hatred.

Facilis descensus averno.

I spoke facing the Canon. "Thank you for your kind introduction." An audible snigger came from an audience member. I turned back to the audience. "If you would allow, I would like to give you an oversight of the organization I work for, and my part within it. After which, I will be happy to take any questions you may have. My name is Liberius. It will come as no surprise to you that this is not my birth name. As I believe some devotees of your monastical orders do, we take new names when we have 'graduated' from our apprenticeships. Our new names are assigned to us. This demonstrates our disregard for our former life and our dedication to our new life."

I was happy with the stony, silent reaction.

"The organization to which I am affiliated is called the Magisterial Association of Diviners. We are not allied to any belief system. If members choose to adopt any mainstream or more off-beat religious practices, that is for their own conscience, but religious tenets do not form part of our work. Personally, I do not associate with any organized religion.

"Our aim is to put order into chaos. We abide by a strict moral code of practice. Those who cannot attain a high level of morality and ethical parameters are not welcome within the organization.

"I have read the documents to which the Reverend Canon has referred, and believe that some of the facts quoted in the texts are flawed. Although I am sure these articles have been written with the best of intentions, with the object of informing the general public of their findings, they are erroneous in their conclusions – at worst deluded.

"These dubious articles have been written by a previous Novitiate of our Association. He could only describe what he thinks he has witnessed, but did not learn the full story prior to putting these into print. It is a shame that had he persevered with the calling, he would have been better placed to report a more accurate account of what we do and how we do it.

"It is my understanding that the author of these accounts has similarly reported on other groups and religious orders, with the same naïveté, having not remained within those groups for an extended period of time, resulting in similar misinformation and conclusive misgivings.

"To my mind, his reporting is similar to asking a seven-year-old child for their perspective on the educational system as a whole, when the child is only able to report from his own, restrictive viewpoint.

"Having said that, there are elements in his reports which do hold true, but again these are biased views without comprehensive explanations or balanced arguments."

I heard the Canon to my left say 'claptrap', but this would have been barely audible to the rest of the assembly. I continued.

"I am open to questions, which I am sure will be legion." A host of hands reached into the air. Oh gosh!

"Thank you. The gentleman in the front row. Please could you state your position and denomination."

The man stood up. "Priest - Church of England. You have not introduced your colleague."

"Apologies – please allow me to introduce you to Stephanus. In short, Stephanus is my superior. As in any other organization, from the Holy Catholic Church to ICI, we adhere to a hierarchical structure. Although Stephanus is in effect my boss, I am designated ambassador for the Association and as such address this esteemed assembly. Stephanus is here for my support and to buy me dinner afterwards."

A little snigger could be heard again from someone in the audience. The Magister Princeps stood and then sat down again without speaking.

"Priest – Church of England. Please can I ask how you came to be involved with your organization?"

I let out a little laugh. "Most certainly, strange as it may seem, I answered a job advertisement in my local newspaper. At the time, I was a shelf-filler in a supermarket and only aged nineteen. I was taken on as a Novitiate and completed six years training before passing my exams to be a designated Adept. It was when I became an Adept, that I assumed the name Liberius – a name which was chosen for me."

The same priest asked a second question. "Could you tell us what your name was before you became Liberius?"

"When I became Liberius, I chose to leave my former life behind. I do use my birth name for legal purposes - my driving license and the such, but it would not be appropriate to disclose my birth name, just as you wouldn't expect a monk or a nun to disclose theirs without a legal reason to do so."

"Priest – Holy Roman Catholic Church. I am surprised that your training took six years to complete. What did you learn in that time?"

"Thank you. Six years' training was only the beginning of my education. I am still learning and still have much to learn. Basic training incorporates herbalism, ethics and a solid grounding in Latin."

The same priest asked "Why Latin?"

"Good question – Latin forms the most difficult element of our training program – to my mind, anyway. I questioned the same thing myself, to be perfectly frank. Latin leaves no room for ambiguity. The Church used Latin for centuries to keep the general population in awe and wonder at the various ceremonies and rites the Church performs. We use Latin for much the same purpose. Some poor souls lost their lives for challenging the use of Latin in the Church. I don't think we would be so harsh if one of our members chose to do the same."

A little titter went up from the audience.

"Sergeant Major – the Salvation Army. You say you studied herbalism. Are you then healers?"

"Thank you. The answer to that is no, we are not healers. Should anyone come to us asking for healing, we direct them to general practitioners. If this is not something they wish to do or if that channel of investigation has been exhausted, we direct them to alternative medicine. On no account do we heal, or attempt to heal the sick. To reiterate – no, we are not healers and do not pretend to be."

The Sergeant Major had a second question. "So why study herbalism if it's not used to heal?"

"Herbs have many varied uses other than for healing. Herbs can alter mood and arouse senses, and combinations of herbs and other natural elements can be used for a multitude of purposes. Some alternative health treatments such as aromatherapy, homoeopathy and naturopathy use some similar techniques. I might be wrong, but I believe the Church uses incense for similar reasons."

"Priest – Church of England. Sorry if I'm a little naïve, but are you a witch? The Reverend Canon described you as such."

"No, I am not a witch. Witches tend to follow a series of religious beliefs, whether they claim to be white or black witches."

(The same questioner). "So, what are you then?"

"I am a warlock – a wizard if you wish. I do not ascribe to any religious beliefs."

(The same questioner again). "What's the difference between a white witch, a black witch and a warlock, then?"

"There is no such thing as a white witch or a black witch - they are both different shades of grey. White witches usually follow some old, pagan religious beliefs, while black witches consider themselves to be devotees of some darker forces. Interestingly, believing in the darker forces demands a belief

231

in the devil, or whatever you choose to call him. To believe in the devil means you have to believe in an opposite power of good. In a bizarre way, believers in the power of Satan also have to believe in the power of Christ. So, to all intents and purposes, devotees of the devil are actually twisted Christians, but fighting for the opposing side. Sorry if that definition was a little long-winded. In short - I am a warlock, using age-old techniques to put order into chaos. I have no religious beliefs or leanings."

(The same questioner again). "So, you are not opposed to the Church or to God?"

"I have no cause to be. I am not on an opposing side. The wisdom I use (and the organization I represent) has no religious or belief foundation. I do not believe in God, but I am certainly not opposed to the belief or anyone who believes."

"Priest – Holy Roman Catholic Church. The reports we have read state that you communicate with the dead. I think we all want to know if this is something you profess to do."

"The short answer to this is a resounding 'no'. It is not possible to communicate with anyone who is no longer alive. Should anyone claim to do so, you would be best to challenge them. But this is the short answer and I think you deserve a better answer than that. We commune with spirits. Spirits are not the spirits of dead people. Spirits are very much alive but do not have the same physical characteristics or tangible features of a corporeal human being. Spirits come in all shapes and sizes - some are helpful, some are mischievous, some of them think themselves as being superior and some of them lie. Take any group of people, the same characteristics apply."

(The same priest). "So, what is the use of communing with spirits? Is it to tell the future? You describe yourselves as 'diviners'?"

"Spirits can give us guidance when our position or a circumstance is unclear. They can advise, but taking them up on their advice is optional. It is possible to determine a likely sequence of events, but we are not fortune-tellers. For instance, and to use your own phraseology, if such-and-such continues on their current path, they are liable for eternal damnation. You are not telling the future, but the likely outcome of events. Does that make sense? Similarly, if a juvenile delinquent continues on their path of criminality they will end up on the wrong side of the law and will end up in prison. In this sort of situation, a spirit could be questioned about what the cause of the problem might be, and perhaps a suitable solution. As I've said previously, we put order into chaos. To be a 'diviner' implies that following a series a patterns as I have already described, a possible outcome can be deduced."

"Minister – United Reformed Church. You speak eloquently and with a well-rounded education. Please can I ask if you are university-educated, if you have been a student of theology and also, why did you choose to become a warlock? It seems an odd profession for a man of your abilities."

"Thank you for that and thank for your kind appraisal of my poor attempt to explain my profession to you. I am a child of the modern comprehensive system. I sat five 'O' levels and passed four of them. I have never been to university or even sixth form for that matter, and my knowledge of theology is seriously lacking, regrettably. Whether I chose my profession is a very good question. It was my choice to answer the advertisement and it was my choice to accept the Novitiate and to continue with my studies when I seemed to be failing miserably – in particular with the dastardly Latin studies. So, in that respect, I chose this profession – however, it had not been a career choice when discussed with the Careers Advisory Service!"

A snigger or two could be heard which prompted me to continue in this vein.

"I suppose if I were to ask you the same question, although it would be presumptuous of me, I would expect your answer to be that you felt it was a 'calling'. On my first day as a Novitiate, my Magister – my trainer – instructed me to nip down to the shop to get us some sausage rolls as it was past breakfast time and he was hungry. I can only answer your question with another – was it a calling for me to enter the profession or was it a sausage roll for breakfast which made me feel at home and in the right place? I'm afraid I really don't know. Whatever the answer – I have had a good life and have enjoyed my elected profession."

I omitted to tell the assembly about the feelings of isolation, or the lack of family and a 'normal life'.

"Priest – Church of England. I was wondering if you could demonstrate for us something of what you are able to do. I understand if this is not possible."

I smiled broadly and said "I was hoping to give you a demonstration of levitation – but I couldn't get those plans off the ground."

The little sniggers were turning into a few out and out laughs – my Magister's jokes were coming in to their own.

"Sorry about that – I've always been accused of being flippant, and have my father's welts to prove it." A few more giggles could be heard. They (and you, the reader of these pages) need know nothing of my father.

"As I'm sure you realize, I am not a magician, I am not a master of illusion – no pulling rabbits out of hats or sawing women in half. But I will happily show you something of my meagre abilities, if you would so allow me. Would you be so kind to join me here, Sir?" I asked the questioner. "Have no fear, I'm not going to use any hocus-pocus or anything unethical. Please – join me!" I could see the Magister Princeps raise an eyebrow.

I faced the questioner head-on. He was middle-aged, of medium build, and suited my purposes ideally. He looked a little worried.

"Please don't be concerned – I can assure you this will be completely harmless. I think it would be foolhardy of me, in front of these esteemed guests to do anything stupid or which could cause harm. I'll just get you a chair, if you don't mind?"

I took an unused chair from the audience and placed my chair in front of his.

"Reverend Canon – please can I ask if I could borrow a couple of pages of one of these documents [which were left on the lectern] for this purpose?"

He simply waved an arm giving me consent. Some people will always be impossible to dissuade from their opinions, no matter what I said or did. That is the nature of belief.

"Please hold a page in each hand and sit facing me. Are you quite comfortable?"

He said he was. I studied him intently. I could hear assembly members murmuring amongst themselves.

I noted every part of the man. His body language - he was apprehensive – I tried to relax him.

"I promise I'm doing nothing which could harm you."

He answered with a surprising answer: "I can't feel anything yet." This was not what I was expecting to hear. Mind you, I'd never tried this before with the muse knowing I was trying to do something.

"I haven't started yet." A few audience members laughed. "Don't worry – you won't feel anything."

I had a good knowledge of the man – his gait, his deportment, how he held his hands and how he held the papers.

"I'm going to sit behind you, so you won't be able to see me. Just stay as you are, please – there will be nothing untoward going on."

He assented.

I took my chair and sat behind him, facing his back. I assumed his posture. The audience continued with their mumblings. When I had his posture exactly, I raised my empty hand and released an imaginary sheet of paper from it. The priest raised his hand and let go of the sheet of paper. He mumbled something to himself and picked it up off the floor. As he did so, I let go of the imaginary sheet again and watched as his paper fell to the floor again. I kicked out a leg and he followed suit. I released the paper for a third time to a ripple of applause. Who would have thought that playing the 'Copy Cat Game' could have ever been used to such great effect?

I thanked the priest for his assistance and he said "I didn't do anything – I couldn't even hold on to a sheet of paper! What did I do?"

The audience rippled with laughter. "Forgive me," I said. "Would somebody please tell this gentleman what he has done." The priest sat next to him leaned over to whisper to him. The Priest had a look of surprise and confusion on his face.

The Canon still scowled, but I had the distinct feeling I was winning over some of this difficult crowd.

Next to ask a question was the only woman present.

"Priest – Church of England. Are there female warlocks or are they all men?"

"Thank you for your question. For clarity, male warlocks have the title 'Magister'. For example, my title is Magister Legatus – Magister Ambassador. Female warlocks have the title

'Mage', but by and large they prefer to be known as 'Sorceresses'. The word 'Mage' tends to be overheard as 'mange' – not a very flattering title."

A ripple of laughter crossed the audience.

"Perhaps Stephanus could tell us how many Magi there are?"

The Magister Princeps stood up. "Altogether, our organization employs twenty-six Magisters, six of whom are Magi."

"Thank you, Stephanus. Perhaps women are more represented in our organization than they are in yours – judging by the percentage of women priests there are here today!"

Laughter was heard again.

The same woman priest asked again, "Isn't that what they called the Three Wise Men in the Bible – the Magi?"

"I believe so. Perhaps we would be better off using the plural form of 'Mages', but personally, I think 'Magi' sounds a little better. Yes, please, the gentleman in the second row..."

"Priest – the Holy Catholic Church. I read in the reports that you have the potential to kill someone, due to some of the nefarious potions and elixirs you make. Do you refute that?"

"A doctor knows how to cure his patient, but he would also have sufficient knowledge to do just the opposite. Anybody, the esteemed assembly here for instance, has the potential to kill in any means they choose to use, but thanks be to God, none of us has that inclination. Having the knowledge of how to do something does not mean you are going to do it. We are not in the habit of 'knocking off' our clientele."

"Priest – Church of England. Please can I ask how you get paid?"

"Monthly."

It was good to hear the sound of laughter.

"Apologies – there I go again, glib as ever. I know what you mean. Clients pay us for our services – whatever that happens to be. All Magisters – apologies again, Magisters and Magi – have specific charge rates for certain services."

I failed to mention the many donations we receive or those who support our organization with gifts or bequests – that might have given the wrong impression - like donations to political parties.

The same priest had a second question. "How do you get these enquiries – for your services, I mean?"

"Thank you, yes. Word of mouth has a large part to play. Others contact Head Office and the enquiry is filtered down to the appropriate Chapter from there."

"So how does someone contact you who doesn't know how to contact Head Office?"

"Sometimes, we put some cryptic ads in national publications – some prominent magazines and the such. Unfortunately, most of the time we have plenty - if not too much – work on at any one time. We receive copious enquiries, most of which we can't help with, but we do help wherever we can."

"What sort of thing can't you help?"

I let out a little laugh. "Can you help me find my cat? Can you make my sister's husband fall in love with me? Can you give me something to make me beautiful? Where can I buy a magic wand? What poison could I buy off you to shut up my neighbour's dog? – that kind of thing. We answer this kind of enquiry politely and professionally, without decrying the querent's bizarre request. We answer all requests with respect, regardless of the enquiry's content or intent."

"Priest – Chrich of England. Due you intend to answer the accusations made against you in the reports we have seen?"

"The short answer to that is 'no'. To do so would only add fuel to the fire. Some people thrive on argument and that is how they find their audience. Leave such things be – they fizzle out on their own."

Then I shocked the audience by opening my hands as though in an explosion – "Pfff! Up in a puff of smoke!" Several audience members, Stephanus and the Canon jumped. I have the same ability to be dramatic when required.

Questions continued for another half hour or so. When the questions were at an end I said "I would like to thank each and every one of you for attending this assembly. I would particularly like to thank the Reverend Canon for having the foresight to convene this assembly, and for allowing us the opportunity to address your concerns."

I started a round of applause, facing the Canon.

The Canon gestured to two attendees and said "Come with me!" and the three sauntered off into a side room.

Many delegates shook my hand and asked if I had a business card, which I happily gave them. The assembly was over. I hoped I had made the impression the Magister Princeps was after.

Chapter 26

The fall-out from the assembly took both me and Magister Princeps Stephanus by surprise. Several attendees had written papers and magazine articles about it. Each was highly complimentary in nature, and from these we received a plethora of requests and appeals for further information. These were not only from the ecclesiastical sector, but also from television and radio, national publications, authors, journalists and broadcasters. Ignatius had a queue of new applicants.

A mountain of letters was piling up on the Magister Princeps' desk – the administrator was flat out trying to prioritise enquiries and where possible, answer those less crucial. Negative, disparaging and offensive letters were discarded and left unanswered.

The Magister Princeps called me into his office to help him go through the prioritised requests. "Goodness knows what we're going to do with all of these. I've put a job ad out for an administrative assistant – we might have to take on two, truth be told. We just don't have anywhere near enough staff to cope with all this. I blame you!" He laughed after saying that.

"Are there any quieter Chapters from whom we could sequester help?"

"A quieter Chapter? I wish! No, I'm afraid there isn't, not now, anyway. We'll just have to wade through what we can and deal with things on a 'first come - first served' basis. But we have a problem – we've received requests for two television interviews and three radio interviews – we'll have to deal with those pronto – we don't want any negative reviews. I'm afraid I'll have to leave these with you – would you be up for that?"

I said I'd be glad to help, but didn't know if I was adequately qualified to do it.

"If London's any indicator of your abilities, I would say you're more than qualified. Have a look at them, would you, please? See what you think."

I said I would.

"I want to ask you something," he said. "How would you feel about leaving your rooms in Maidstone and taking root here, with us, so to speak? I have enquired about a nearby property – it's only a small cottage, but I think it would suit you admirably. What do you think? I can take you to have a look at it, if you like? You can always say no."

I said I'd be happy to take a look at it. My rooms in Maidstone were of little or no use to me now. I had hardly been there more than three times in the last year – it would make sense to take advantage of Stephanus' kind offer. Letting go of my home would be simple enough, but letting go of my home town would be a different matter. Was I ready for this upheaval? The more I thought about it, the more I came to the realisation that Maidstone was no longer the Maidstone I had known. The haunts of my youth – the pubs, clubs, cafés and shops had now gone. Maidstone to me was now no more than the county town of Kent. 'There's no place like home' and this place felt nothing like home.

"Good," he said. "we'll take a look at the cottage after lunch. Meanwhile, take a gander over these media requests, would you?" He passed me the requests which I took into the conservatory to read through.

The three radio interview requests were similar to each other – general information broadcasts, looking for a local slant to the station's location. One of the television programs was for a day-time news magazine (how a centuries-old profession could be considered to be 'news' was something of an enigma) and the other was a strange suggestion to take part in a TV cookery program. Perhaps I could suggest some 'magic' recipes or could I 'conjure up' something for the program. Perhaps they didn't realise that the nearest I ever came to cooking was shoving something in the microwave hoping it would come out hot and not ruined. I would have to take advice on that – perhaps one of my colleagues could suggest something? I couldn't think of anything at all.

None of these interviews was to be anything like the cross-examination of the assembly and each indicated that I would be given a copy of the interview questions prior to the show's recording. They seemed simple enough, so I wrote accepting the requests.

At lunchtime, Stephanus and I went to view the cottage in the village. It was a lovely little property and beautifully furnished. I accepted the kind offer. I would have to go back to Maidstone to collect any property I didn't want to throw out, and I could do with seeing my mother before the move. I hadn't been in contact for a while, but in reality, neither of us had made an effort in that respect. She was busy with my brother's children and their 'weird uncle' was probably barely mentioned. I couldn't help but wonder what might go through her mind when she saw me on the telly! The mind boggled.

"Did you say you'd see your mother when you go back to Maidstone to get your stuff?" Stephanus asked.

I said that was my plan.

"Ask her to teach you to cook something. If it wasn't for our housekeeper, we'd all starve here."

I said it was a good idea – if my mother was congenial enough. She had made some lovely pastries in the past, but these were probably way out of my abilities in the kitchen.

"I'll go tomorrow," I told Stephanus. "Will that be OK? I need to give notice on my rooms."

"Fine with me," he said. "I'll get the contract signed on the cottage so it will be ready for you to move in when you get back. Let me know when you're going return, please."

I left for Maidstone the following morning, having agreed to meet my landlord the next day.

A mound of post lay against the inside of my front door. Mountains of junk mail, freebie newspapers, charity bags and vouchers for replacement windows and doors, which I neither needed nor wanted. Small wonder the rainforests were being depleted.

I sorted the wheat from the chaff while the kettle boiled, putting the junk mail in the bin and the rest by my armchair in the sitting room to peruse with a cup of tea. I had no milk, so had to drink the tea black. A small sacrifice for the joy of reading bills, bills and more bills!

A handwritten envelope with my brother's handwriting gave me some sense of foreboding. Dated four weeks previously, the letter informed me that following a short illness (not specified) my mother had died. The date of the funeral at Vinters Park Crematorium had taken place two days ago. He apologised for not being able to contact me in any other way and he had no idea of my whereabouts. He gave his phone number to contact him, which I did.

He had some nick-nacks from my mother's house he thought I might like, and he told me the contents of my mother's will. She had left everything to my two nephews – but this did not amount to very much.

I thanked him for informing me and I apologised to him that I had not been a more dutiful son and brother. I told him of my imminent move and arranged to pick up the few items from him the following afternoon.

Next day, I sorted out my affairs and collected the bits and pieces from my brother. He did not invite me in as they were about to go shopping. I left him a telephone number to contact me on, should the need arise. That was the last time I saw my brother.

Within the week, I had sorted out that which needed sorting and I made my way back to the MAD House. My time in Maidstone and my previous life had come to an end, and I felt strangely happy in that knowledge.

///

The cottage in the village suited my purposes very nicely. A lick of paint here and a dab or two of bleach there was all the house needed to become comfortable. A few Magisters joined me for a celebratory drink a day or two after I'd settled in, and then we were down to the pressing business of the day.

It was 2003 and Stephanus had a computer installed in the MAD house – I could only just manage a typewriter and had no computer knowledge whatsoever. One of the new administrators gave me a bit of a crash course, but I couldn't see how this new system would be of any benefit to me. I left the working of it to the administrators, as did Stephanus and the majority of the Magisters.

With the new computer system, applications, requests and general enquires came flooding in. A mobile office (which was intended to be temporary but became permanent) was put in the grounds of the building. This is located next to Central Stores, for anyone who is not familiar with the layout of the place.

For the time being, I concentrated on the media enquiries and had my own Novitiate. We travelled the country together – my Novitiate acting as general assistant. It bothered me that she had little time for her studies or practical work, so I gave her a planned study regime. I made sure that she became fully proficient in the identification and uses of herbs.

The housekeeper gave me a surefire recipe for a cheese and sausage roll, which I made for the cookery programme. To my great amusement and that of the other Magisters, a review in a newspaper said I was a 'wizard in the kitchen'. I didn't accept any further cookery programs, though.

Unlike me, my Novitiate excelled in her Latin studies and had a good memory for symbols and potions. In between her education and our travels, she became very clever on the computer and she introduced me to the benefits of using email. It became apparent that this electronic system of sending messages was much more proficient than using the postal system. Albeit, I still preferred the old methods and have never quite taken to using the computerised system.

The whole organisation was becoming more regimented and less disorganised. And then my Novitiate left. It left me in a difficult situation as I was not proficient enough to use the computer to retrieve all the data which was on it. I gave Ignatius a call and he came to the MAD house so that he could determine what I needed in a Novitiate.

It was good to see him. We chatted for a long time – he caught me up on his life. He had been tasked with setting up some kind of a Novitiate school and was currently looking for a suitable premises. We chewed the fat long into the night. "You really ought to write it all down," he said, "your life, I mean. Perhaps if you were to produce a record of your life and what you have achieved, it could encourage others. Besides all that, I think there would be a lot of people interested."

I said I'd give it some thought. He suggested I took a course in computing for seniors. "Don't look at me like that – we're no spring chickens. You're even older than me! You must be pushing fifty! Haven't you noticed?"

He was right. It was now 2005 and I was just two years away from turning fifty. I didn't feel middle-aged but understanding modern technology made me feel old. Just as I was left behind in my recollections of my home town, I felt I was getting left behind in this modern world. Old age creeps up on us without us realising it.

"Make a few notes, at least," he suggested. "I'm sure we can find a ghost writer for you if you don't feel up to it."

I said I'd give it my consideration.

I was sad to see him go. I would say we had become like brothers, but considering my relationship with my own brother, that analogy seems flawed.

Ignatius arranged for an Adept with the given name of Callixtus to help me with my work. He was a very able young man and had no trouble keeping me organised. Callixtus agreed with Ignatius that it would be a good idea to jot down a few of my memories. He said he would be happy to help if he could. I said to him as I said to Ignatius, that I would give it some thought.

Truthfully, I sincerely doubted that anyone would be interested in reading anything about my life. I could be proven wrong, but it would be a lot of work to have it fall flat and come to nothing. My time might be better spent doing the work I was called to do.

We were going about our usual business when Stephanus called into our Sanctum to speak to me.

"Have you got a minute?" he asked. "Something's come in I want you to take a look at."

I followed him into the conservatory. He asked the housekeeper to bring us some tea.

"I just want to run something past you," he said. Stephanus usually spoke at a rate of knots, but now he was speaking slowly, carefully considering each word he spoke. I sensed I was either in trouble or changes were coming. I did hope he wasn't going to ask me to write my memoirs like everyone else seemed to be doing.

I tried to be a little light-hearted. "I'm all ears," I said, flapping my hands at the side of my ears like a demented elephant. There was me – forever flippant.

"Good," he said, without laughing. "We have received a very...unusual request from a very...unusual source. Should you decide or feel that this assignment is not for you, all well and good. But I would like you to consider it all the same." He took a sip of tea. "When I received this...request, my first reaction was to reject it. However, with careful consultation with the spirits, I believe it would be in our best interests to accept."

I did wish he could have got to the point a bit quicker. This was more tense than watching a Hitchcock movie.

"To accept this assignment, there will be a change in your circumstances – I mean, you would have to step down from the work you are currently involved with. This will be a highly clandestine project. Currently, your work is more...public, more...open, if you like. This would be a big change."

He looked uncomfortable.

"Not to beat about the bush (!), we have received an application for help from a very...high-powered...prominent source. Not to put too fine a point on it, we have received a request from the Vatican!"

That was not what I was expecting. I was expecting maybe a politician or a police commissioner – something like that. But the Vatican?

He continued, cautiously. "I need not tell you that this...project and any discussions about it are strictly 'entre-nous'. It cannot be discussed with anyone outside of this room. Should you agree to take this on, you will simply have to 'disappear' for the duration of the mission."

I said I understood the need for secrecy. I asked him what the mission would involve.

"The Vatican is in crisis. Several priests and even some higher authorities – Cardinals - have been accused of some dire…improprieties. Our help has been requested to determine if there is any foundation to these accusations."

I said that I believed the Vatican had their own investigators – why should they need our help?

"Yes, the inquisitors. Unfortunately, some inquisitors have also been implicated in misdoings. As our work is covert in nature, they have decided that we would be best able to investigate and report our findings without anyone being any the wiser that the investigations are even being conducted. What do you think?"

I said it wouldn't be something I could give an answer to without careful consideration and consultation, but secretly relished the challenge.

"If you were to go – I'm afraid you would need to be located in the Vatican itself. You would not be able to take Callixtus with you, but you could use some of his free time to write your memoirs for you. You can communicate by email. Apologies – Ignatius told me about his suggestion for you to do so. I think it would be a very good idea, by the way. Do you have a passport?"

I said I didn't. "Of course, you would have to travel under your given name, but when on site I would advise that you use the moniker of Father Nicholas again.

I said that last time I used that, I was questioned about how I came by that title.

"That's easily mended," he said. "There was an order of monks many years ago, who went by the name of the Trinitarians.

Father Nicholas is the last of the Trinitarians – the order has been incorporated into other orders. It would be a good idea to supply you with a habit – let's make this as credible as possible."

"Would it be best if I shaved my head?" I asked the question but hoped for a negative response.

Stephanus laughed. "No – I think that might be going a bit too far. You might think about growing a beard though, but only if you feel like it."

I said I wished he had given me these suggestions before. Such moves would have given me much better cover than just travelling incognito in my usual casual clothing. I started thinking of this as not so much deceit as camouflage.

"Take some time. Should you decide to take the assignment, you are free to inform Callixtus that you have some work to do away from home and you can keep in touch with him. He will be none the wiser as to where you are or what you are doing."

I said I would consider the proposal and take some advice from the spirits.

"Navigating the inner workings of the Vatican will require a lot of information and intuition. Eusebius will be invaluable to you. Ask him for his advice, please."

I said I would and left Stephanus to finish his tea. I did consider the proposal and did converse with Harry and Eusebius, who were falling over themselves to help me. I told Stephanus that evening that I would be happy to take on this most sensitive of missions.

I was on the brink of a new chapter in my life. Whether I was the right person for the job or not was something I was going to have to find out on my own.

I might succeed, I might fail. A shelf-stacker from a mini-market on the Sandling Road in Maidstone was heading for the Vatican.

Facilis descensus averno.

END